DRAGON BALL

Let the Tournament Begin!

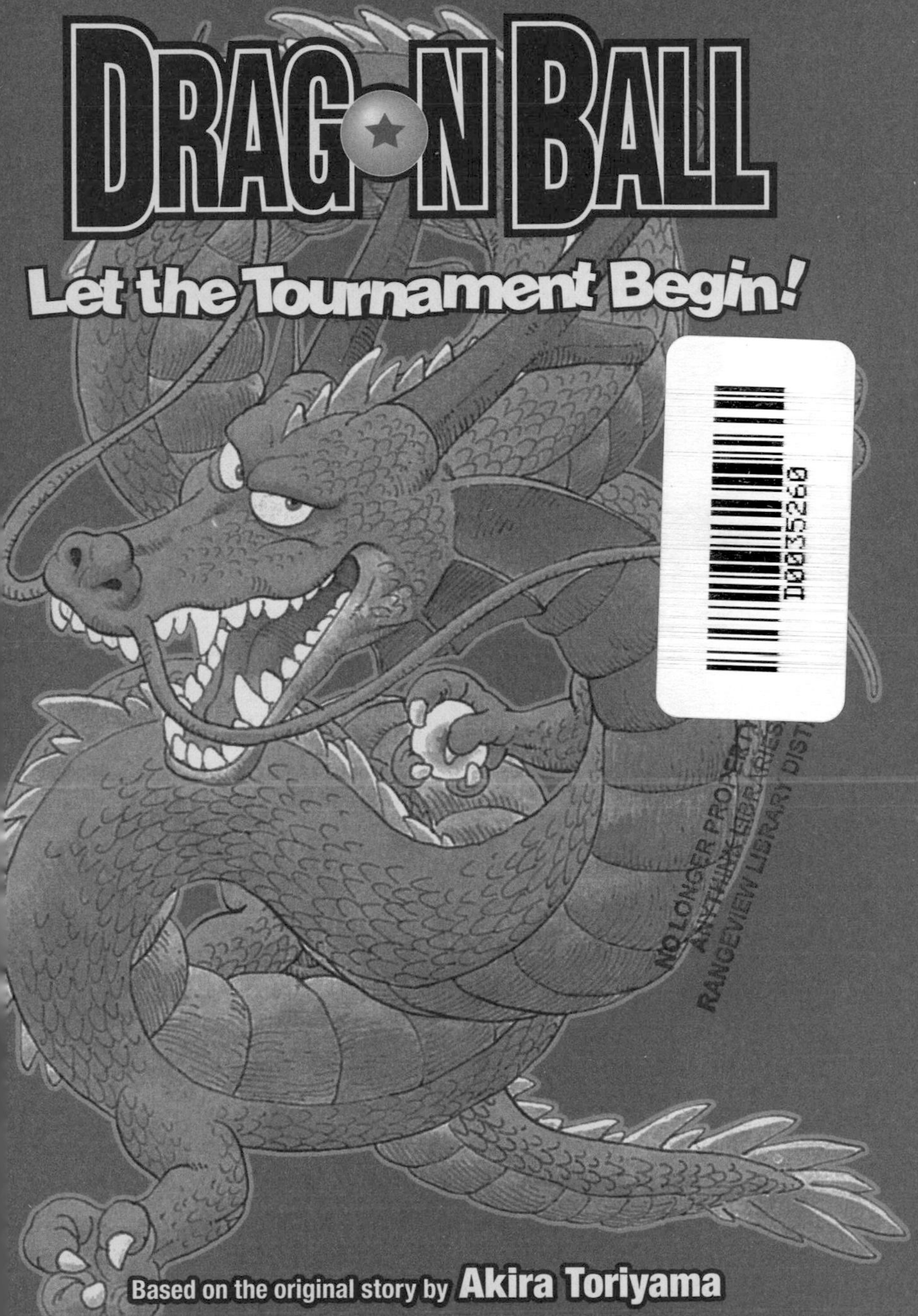

Based on the original story by **Akira Toriyama**

Adapted by Gerard Jones

DRAGON BALL LET THE TOURNAMENT BEGIN!
CHAPTER BOOK 7

Illustrations: Akira Toriyama
Design: Frances O. Liddell
Coloring: ASTROIMPACT, Inc.
Touch-Up: Frances O. Liddell & Walden Wong
Original Story: Akira Toriyama
Adaptation: Gerard Jones

DRAGON BALL © 1984 by BIRD STUDIO. All rights reserved.
Original manga first published in Japan in 1984 by SHUEISHA Inc., Tokyo.
This English language chapter book novelization is based on the original manga.

Sources for page 78, "A Note About Bacterian":

"Hygiene Promotion." *Global Water, Sanitation and Hygiene (WASH).* Centers for Disease Control and Prevention.
http://www.cdc.gov/healthywater/global/sanitation/hygiene_promotion.html (Accessed October 7, 2009)

"Body Lice." Centers for Disease Control and Prevention.
http://www.cdc.gov/lice/body/index.html (Accessed October 7, 2009)

"Ringworm." *Water Related Diseases.* World Health Organization.
http://www.who.int/water_sanitation_health/diseases/ringworm/en/ (Accessed October 7, 2009)

"Trachoma." Centers for Disease Control and Prevention.
http://www.cdc.gov/ncidod/dbmd/diseaseinfo/trachoma_t.htm (Accessed October 7, 2009)

"Scabies." Centers for Disease Control and Prevention.
http://www.cdc.gov/scabies/ (Accessed October 7, 2009)

"Sweating and Body Odor." CNN Health.com.
http://www.cnn.com/HEALTH/library/sweating-and-body-odor/DS00305.html (Accessed October 7, 2009)

"Basics." *Sweating and Body Odor.* Mayo Clinic.com.
http://www.mayoclinic.com/health/sweating-and-body-odor/DS00305/DSECTION=causes (Accessed October 7, 2009)

Printed in the U.S.A.

Published by
VIZ Media, LLC
P.O. Box 77010
San Francisco, CA 94107

10 9 8 7 6 5 4 3 2 1
First printing, March 2010

www.vizkids.com   www.viz.com

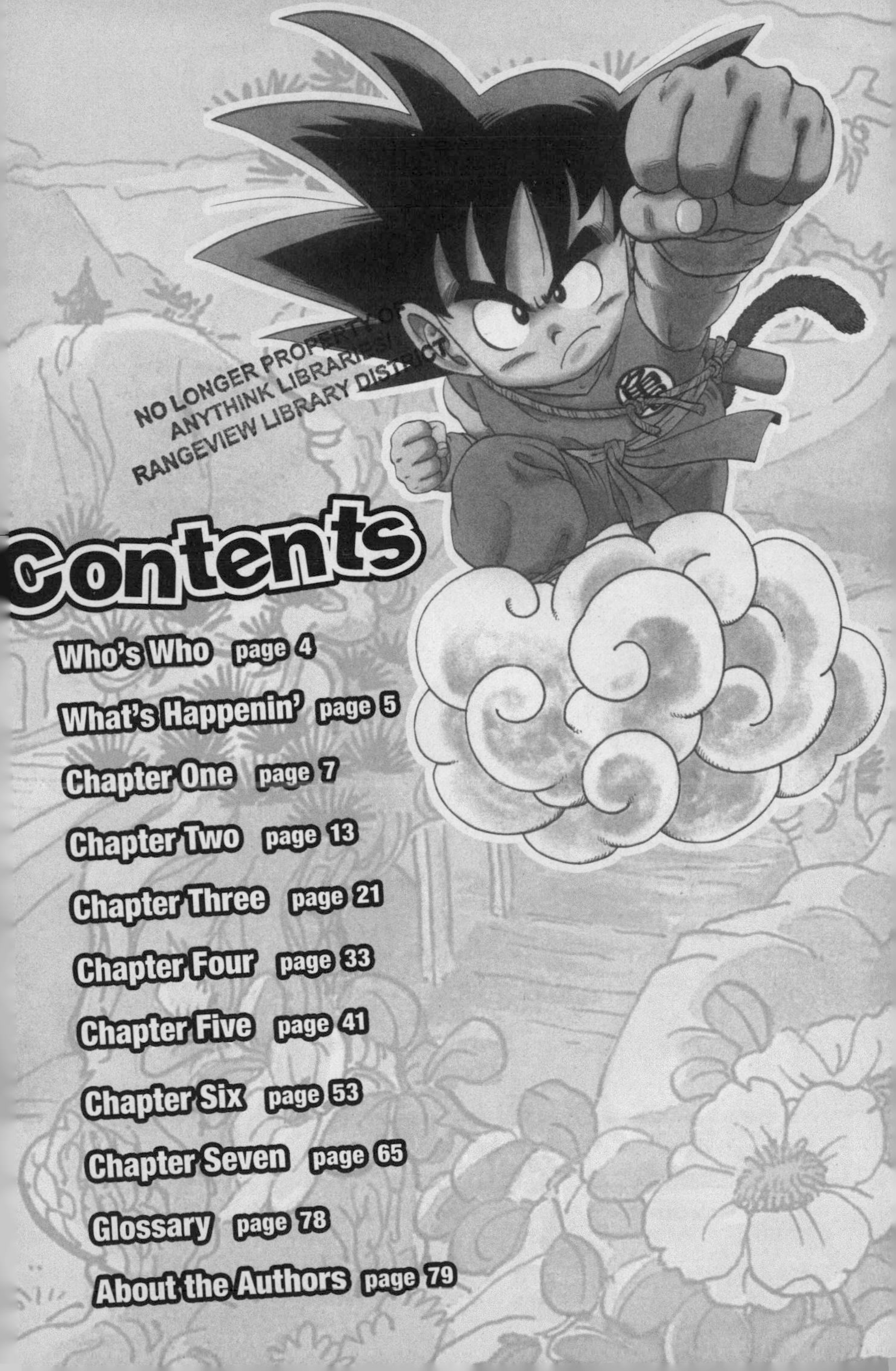

Contents

Who's Who

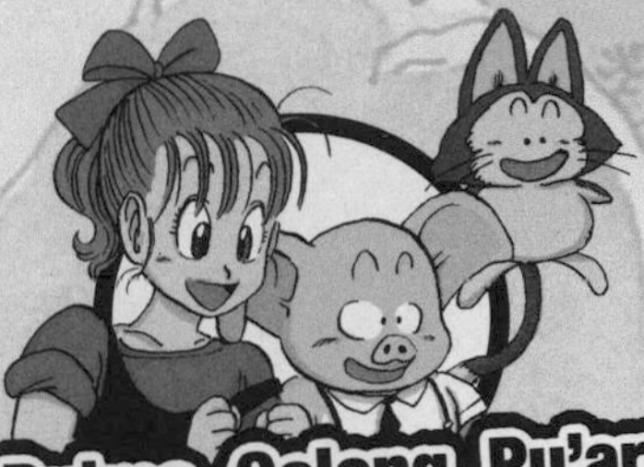

Bulma, Oolong, Pu'ar

It's Goku's old friends from the days of the Dragon Ball quest! Now they're living in the city, and Oolong has finally taken the underpants off his head.

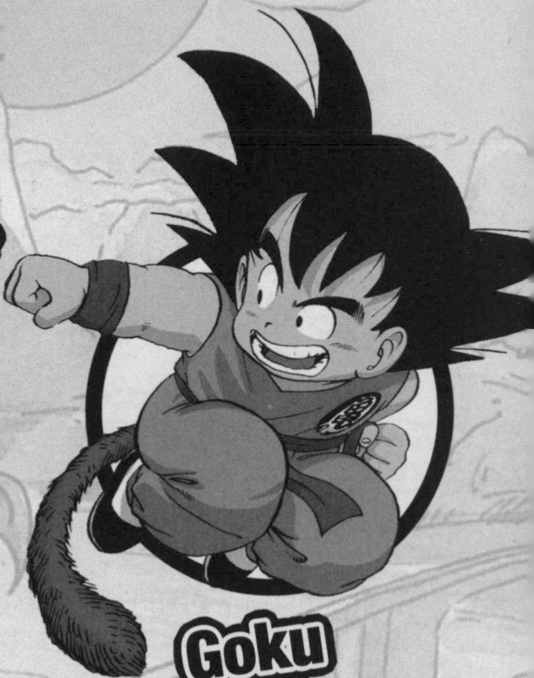

Goku

This kid's come a long way since his days of forest living. He's become quite a warrior with the strength of a big, hairy, apelike beast...and a heart of gold.

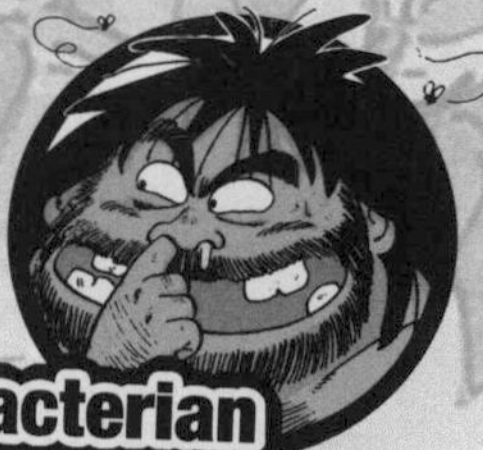

Bacterian

Hold your nose! Bacterian's one funky fighter. If his smell doesn't knock you out cold, he'll get you with his Stink-Fu!

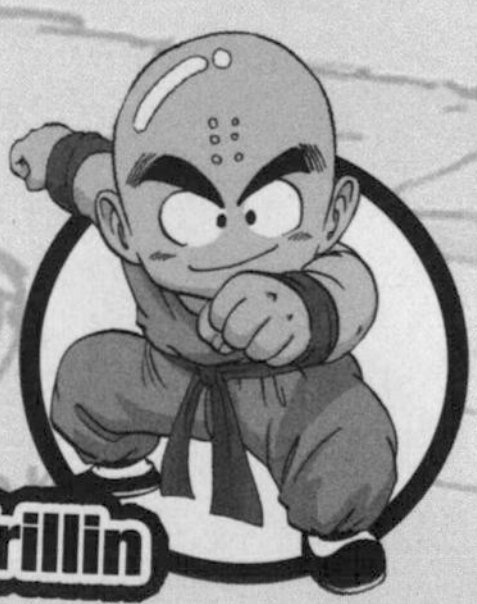

Krillin

This little baldie was full of mischief when he first arrived on Master Roshi's island, but now he and Goku are the best of friends.

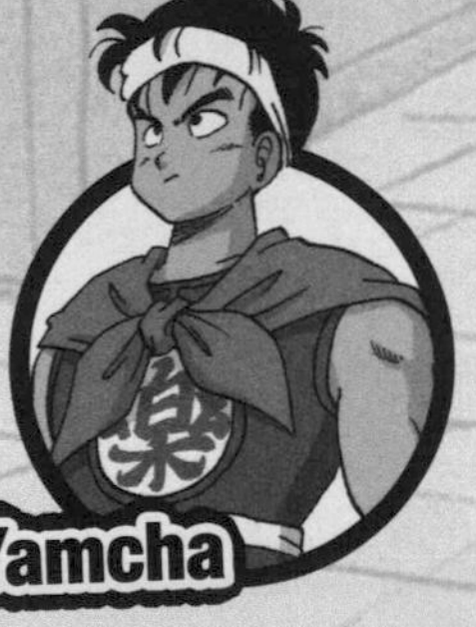

Yamcha

The bad boy of the desert is back! And this time he's looking a little more tame. He may have lost his bark, but does his Fist of the Wolf Fang still have its bite?

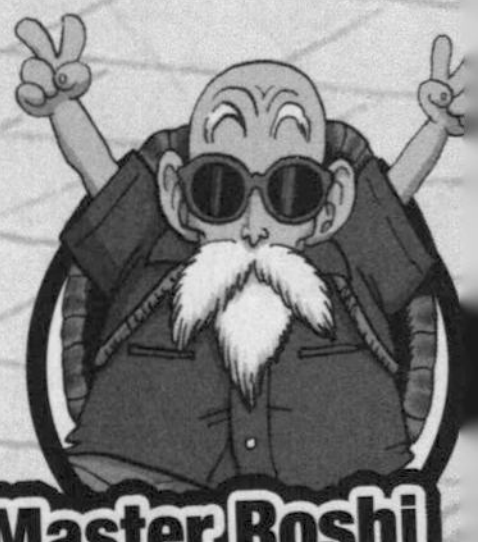

Master Roshi

a.k.a. Turtle Guy

Master Roshi may look like a harmless old man, but behind that mustache he packs a serious Kame-Hame-Ha!

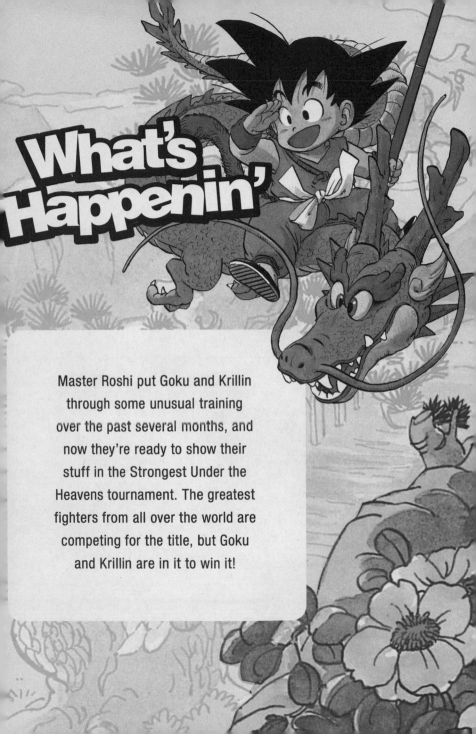

What's Happenin'

Master Roshi put Goku and Krillin through some unusual training over the past several months, and now they're ready to show their stuff in the Strongest Under the Heavens tournament. The greatest fighters from all over the world are competing for the title, but Goku and Krillin are in it to win it!

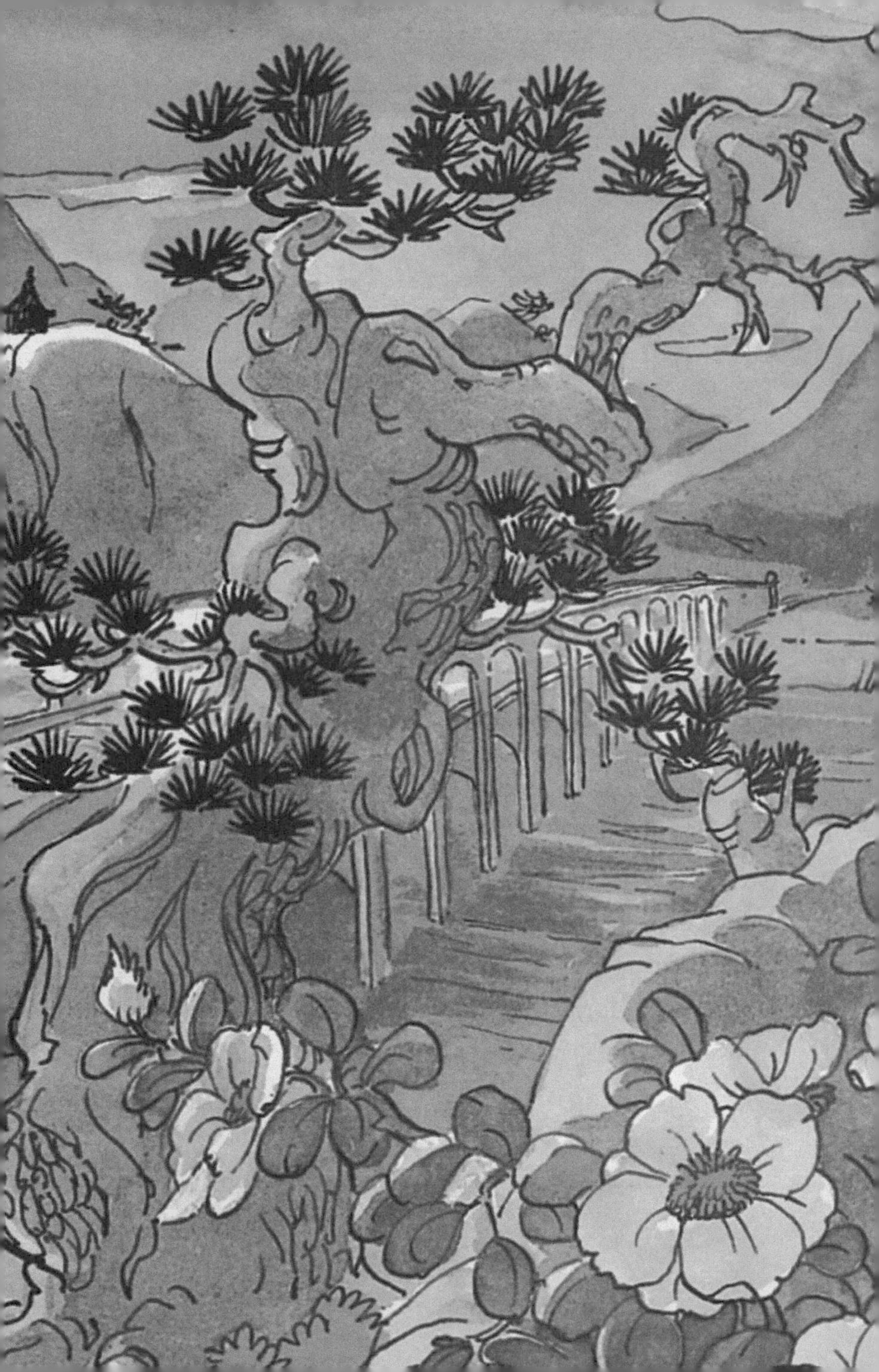

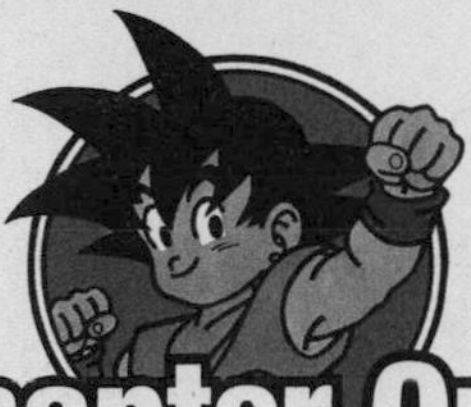

Chapter One

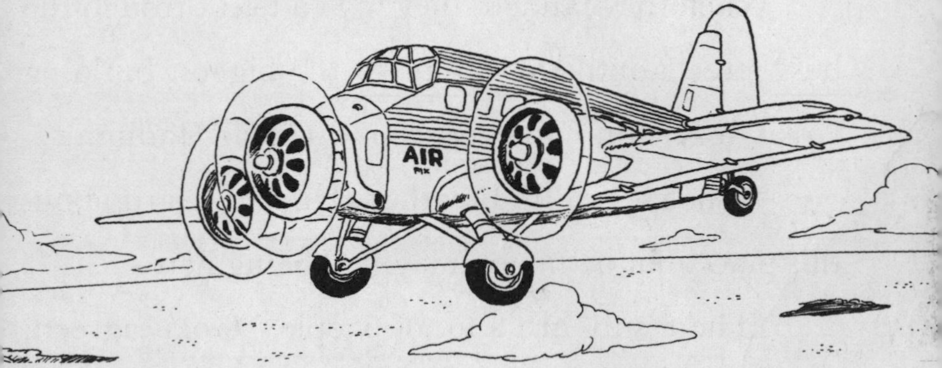
AIR

Goku had never been on an airplane before. "I can't believe this big metal thing can actually fly," he said as he clicked his seatbelt closed. "It really *can* fly!" he cried when they were in the air. "But it's a lot slower than Kinto'un."

In the seat next to him Krillin rolled his eyes and sighed. It had taken him a while to get used to Goku, but after months of training side by side, they had become pretty good friends. Now Master Roshi was taking them to the Southern Metropolis to compete in the most awesome martial arts tournament in the world: The Tenkaichi Budokai, also known as "Strongest Under the Heavens."

When they landed, they took a taxi through the busy streets until they came to the biggest building Goku or Krillin had ever seen: Budokai Stadium.

"Whoa," Krillin breathed. He had heard about this place, but he never imagined being here.

"There sure are a lot of people," Goku agreed, looking around.

"Yeah," Krillin replied. "And I'm starting to get a little nervous."

"Around the corner," the man at the registration table said as Master Roshi and the boys approached. "You can get your tickets there."

"You don't understand," Roshi said. "We're not spectators. These two are here to compete."

"*What*?!" the man gasped, gazing wide-eyed

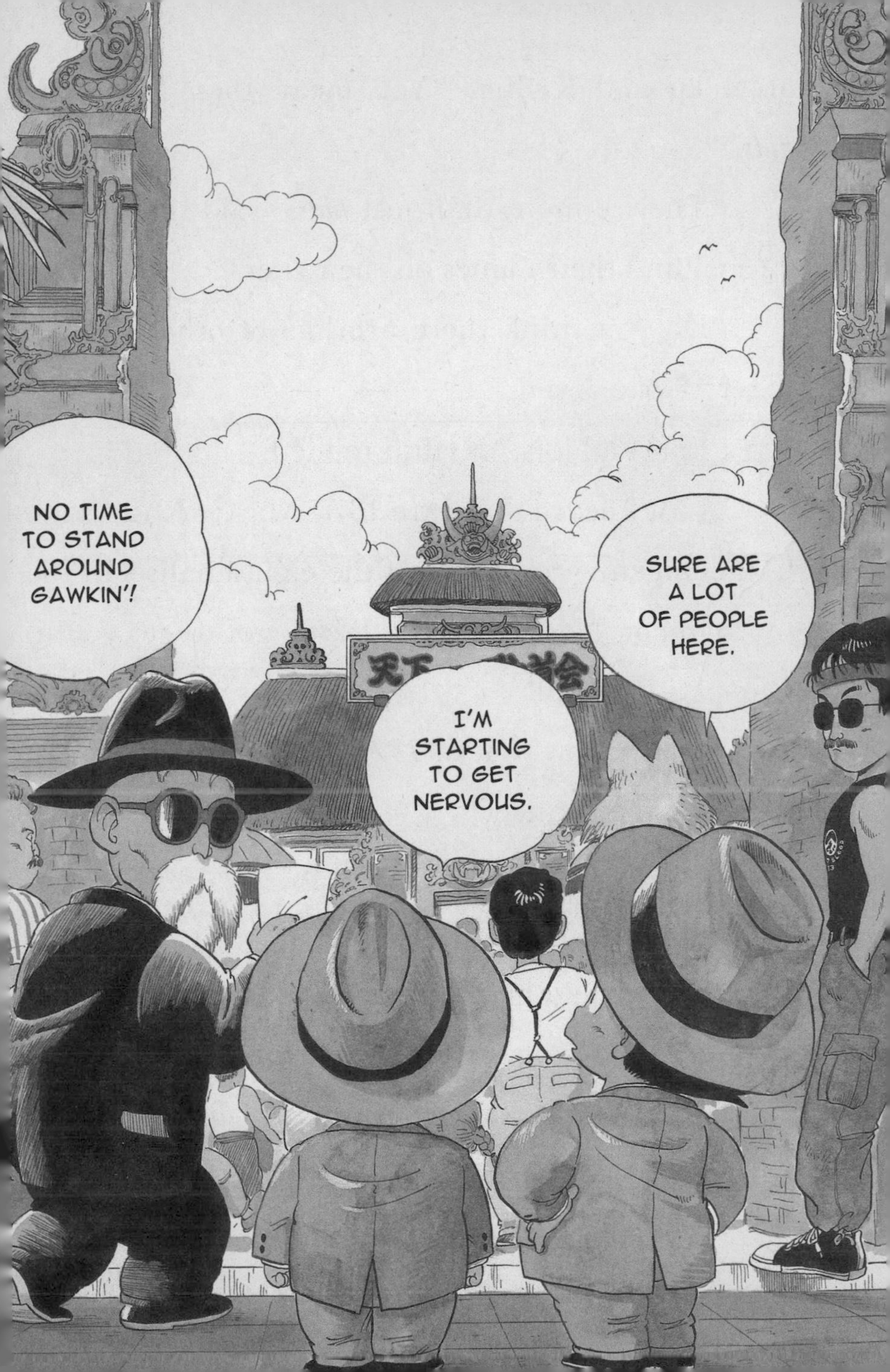
SURE ARE A LOT OF PEOPLE HERE.
I'M STARTING TO GET NERVOUS.
NO TIME TO STAND AROUND GAWKIN'!

at Goku and Krillin. "You mean these two little *kids*?!"

"They're more than just *kids*," said the master. "You'll find their names on the roster."

"Do you think there are lots of other fighters here?" Goku asked.

"Lots and lots," Krillin replied.

"Last I heard there are 137," Master Roshi said. "All competing to be one of the eight finalists in the tournament. Now come on! We've got to get you to Competition Hall!"

"Only eight...out of *137*?" Krillin gasped. "We don't stand a chance!"

"Maybe most of them will be little and weak," Goku said.

But all the other fighters looked big and strong. In fact, the only ones who looked small were Krillin and Goku. Among the many, many, *many* creatures, Goku and Krillin were the smallest of them all.

"Y-you know," Krillin said, "I wonder if we'd do

better if we waited for the *next* tournament..."

"That would be a shame," Master Roshi said, "since I had these made *especially* for you."

He reached into his suitcase and pulled out two orange uniforms, each with the Japanese character for "turtle" written on the chest.

"For...for us?" Krillin cried. "Real *gi*, like real martial artists wear?"

"You *are* real martial artists," the master smiled.

"I'll do my best to be worthy of this honor," Krillin bowed.

"This is great!" Goku cried. "Much better than those monkey suits you made us wear." He tore his suit off, right in front of everybody, and put his uniform on.

"Now get in there and do your best!" the master said. "I'll be out front—and hoping to see you both in the finals!"

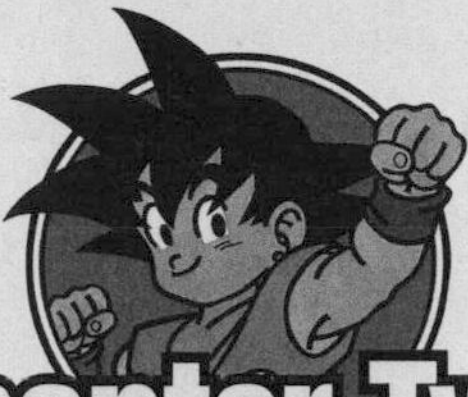

Chapter Two

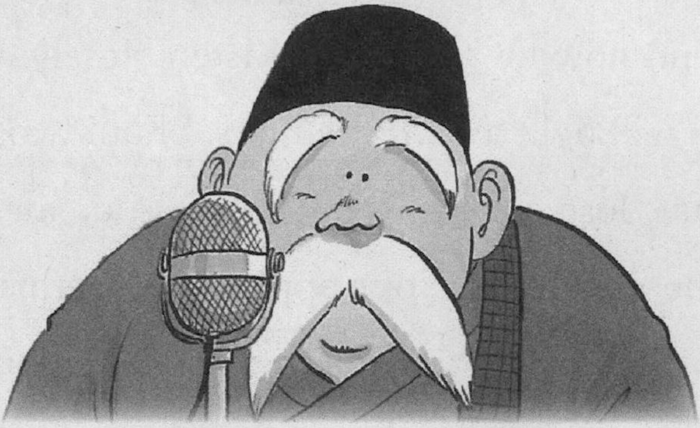

An elderly man shuffled up to the microphone in the center of the arena. He cleared his throat, and a hush fell over the crowd.

"Welcome, contestants!" he said in a thin voice. "For five years you have trained hard and waited patiently for the opportunity to compete in this tournament–"

"Have we trained for five years?" Goku whispered.

"Not even close," Krillin replied.

"–Well, the day has finally arrived. This year we have a total of 137 masters from all corners of the earth. Only eight will be allowed to enter the final rounds. The competition will be very fierce indeed.

"And now for the rules. Listen closely. All contestants will fight atop these mats. Should you fall off your mat, lose consciousness, or beg for mercy, you lose. You may injure your opponent, but this is not a fight to the death. You may not use weapons. Each qualifying round will last only one minute. If the match has not been settled in that time, the judges will determine the winner.

"Because we have so many contestants, you will each draw a number to determine your matches. Best of luck to you all!"

The contestants lined up to choose their numbers. Based on their numbers they were grouped into one of four "blocks." Each block was assigned a mat, and the members of that block would battle each other until only two fighters from each block were left. Those remaining eight would fight in the final rounds.

"I got number 93," Krillin said, looking at his piece of paper. "What'd you get, Goku?"

"It looks like a pelican and a ball," Goku said, squinting at his paper.

"Give me that!" Krillin said. "That's 70. But that means..." He looked at the chart on the wall that showed which numbers were in which block. "Agh! We're in the same block! That means we might have to fight each other!"

"But our numbers are pretty far apart, right?" Goku said, trying to figure out the chart. "Maybe they won't match us up right away."

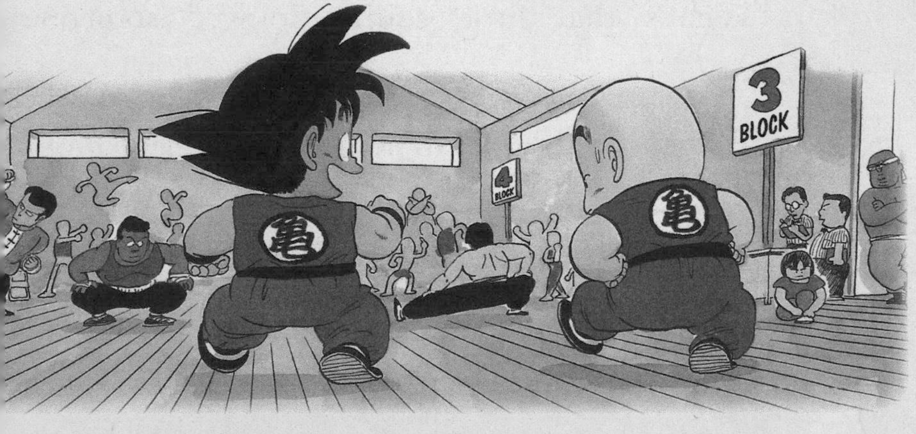
3
BLOCK
4
BLOCK

Krillin sighed. "And since I'm bound to get knocked out by the first guy I fight, I guess it doesn't really matter anyway."

Goku laughed. "You'll be fine! Just do everything the Turtle Guy taught us!"

"Like what?" Krillin moaned. "He never taught us to fight!"

Just then, a referee climbed onto one of the mats. "Block 3, let's begin!" he shouted. "Numbers 69 and 70!"

"Guess that's me," Goku said as he climbed onto the mat.

The audience roared with laughter when they realized Goku was about to fight.

"What's that little squirt doing?" someone laughed.

"Whoever's about to fight him is one lucky guy," someone else giggled.

"Good luck, Goku!" Krillin cried.

A huge man stepped onto the mat opposite

Goku. "Whot ees dees?!" he bellowed. "Dere ees no joy in croshing soch an ant!"

"Oh yeah?" Goku said, crouching low. He set his face with a look of determination.

"You have one minute!" cried the ref. "Go!"

Goku rushed at his opponent. He dashed between the man's legs before the man knew what was happening.

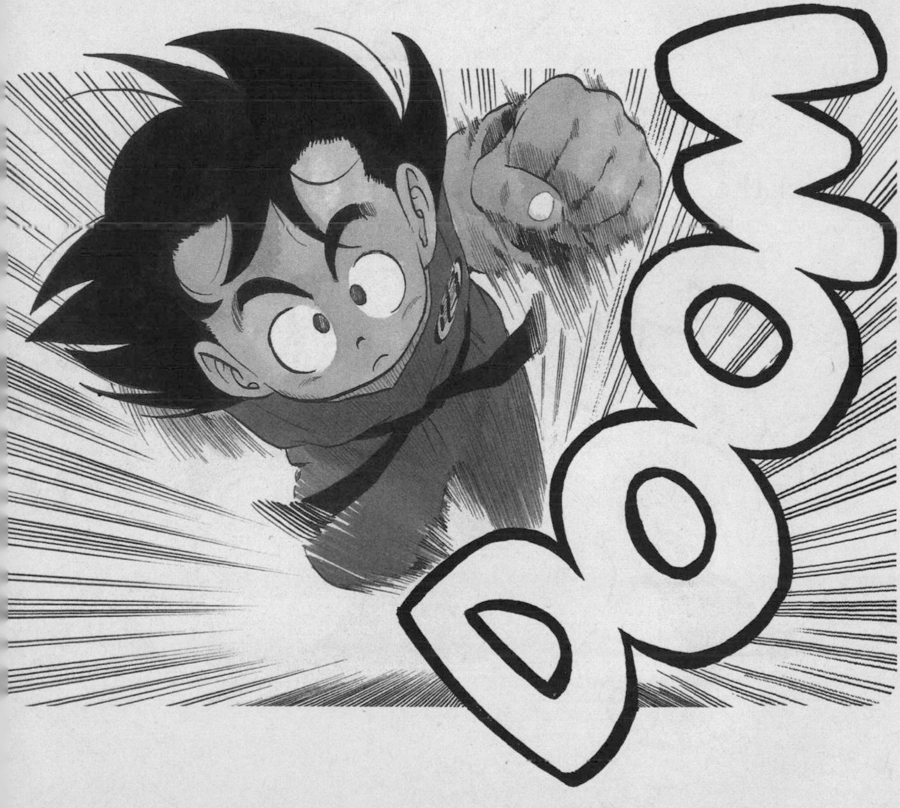
DOOM

"Whot?" the man said, looking around. "He vanishes?!"

"Yoo hoo!" Goku called. With a single finger he tapped the man to get his attention.

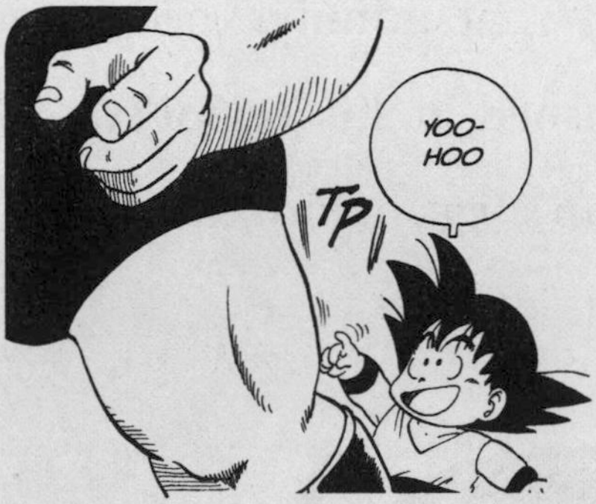
YOO-
HOO
TP

At the touch of Goku's finger, the man toppled over the side of the mat and fell like a tree.

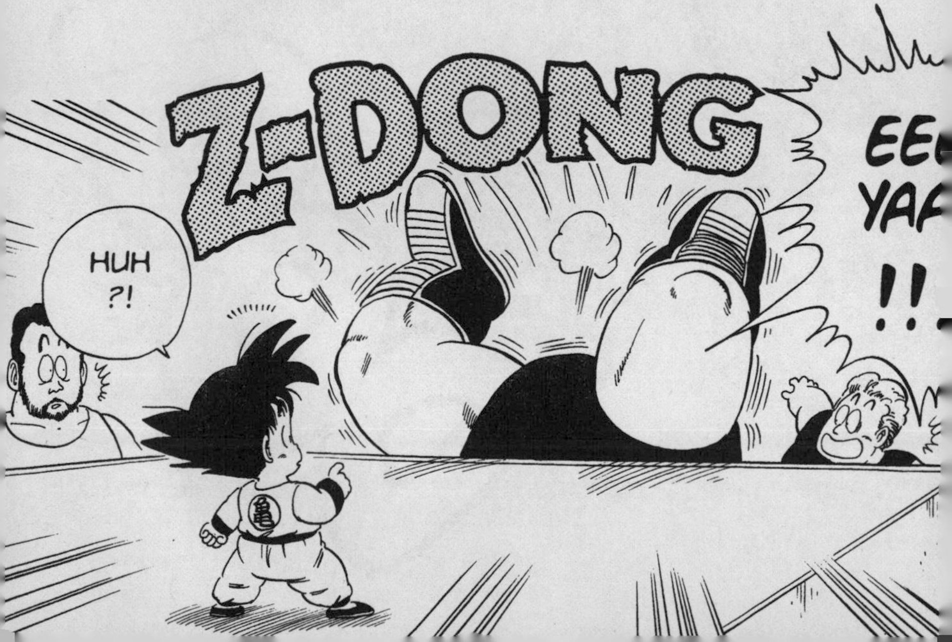
Z-DONG
HUH
?!

"Huh?" Goku breathed, his finger still poised mid-tap.

Everyone—the other contestants, the referee, Goku, and the giant man—was too stunned to move. (Although, strictly speaking, the giant man wasn't moving because he was barely conscious.) Then the referee's hand shot up.

"V-v-victory!" he stammered. "To number 70!"

"W-what just happened?!" yelled one of the other fighters.

"Aw, he musta lost his balance and fell," sneered another.

"Y-yeah," said a third. "Th-that must be it." And he forced himself to laugh.

"Man, what luck!" Krillin said to Goku as he climbed down from the mat. "Who'd have thought that guy would trip and fall?!"

Goku just stared at his hand for a moment. "Uh-uh," he mumbled. "That's not it."

"What's not it?" Krillin asked.

Goku thought for a minute. "Krillin, listen!" he said suddenly. "Unless your opponent's really, really strong—*don't* put all of your strength into your blows!"

"What the heck are you—?" Before Krillin could finish, he heard a voice that made him freeze.

"Well, well, well! If it isn't my old friend Krillin!"

Krillin turned around—and went pale with fear.

Chapter Three

WHAT ?!

"What's new, Krillin?" the fighter sneered as he approached. "I haven't seen you since you ran away crying from Orin Temple."

His friend grinned. "Don't tell us you're trying out for the *tournament*, crybaby!"

"W-w-well," Krillin mumbled, his confidence slipping away. "I j-just thought…"

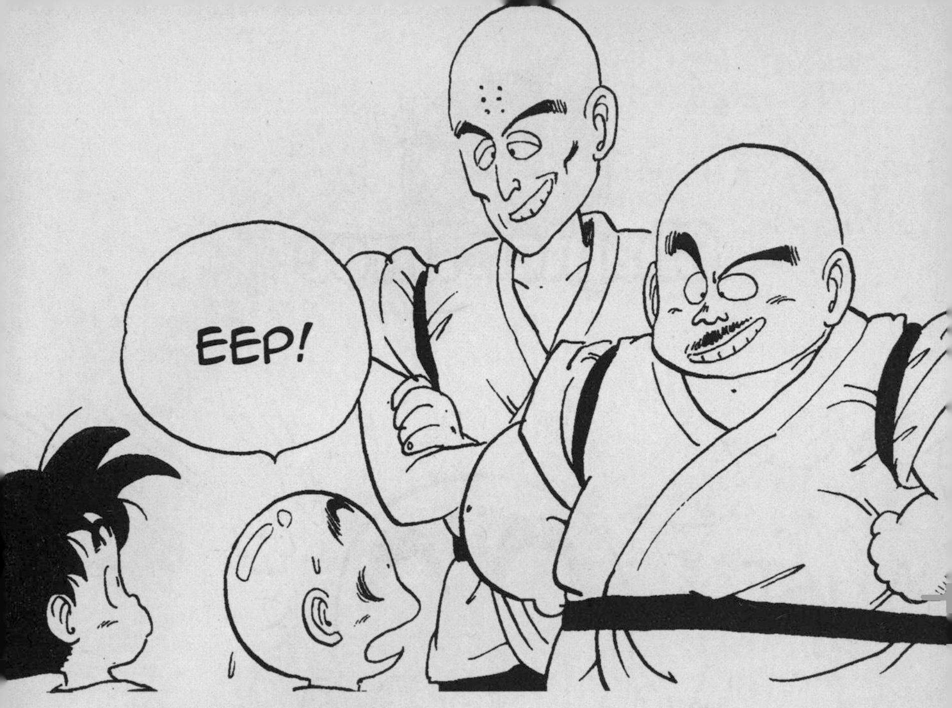
EEP!

The taller one snatched the piece of paper out of Krillin's hand. "Ha! Lucky me!" he laughed. "*You're* my first opponent!"

"*What*?" Krillin gasped. He couldn't believe his bad luck.

"Just promise me one thing, Krillin," the tall one said.

"W-what's that?"

"Promise you won't *hurt* me!" He and his friend walked away laughing.

"Those guys didn't seem very nice," Goku said, watching them leave.

Krillin stared at the floor. "Yeah. They used to bully me at my old martial arts school. Well," he sighed. "That's that. Now I *know* I don't have a chance!"

"Listen, Krillin..." Goku frowned. "When you fight this guy, strike with all the strength you've got!" A mischievous smile spread across his face.

"B-but you just said..."

"Forget about that," Goku grinned. "Just get out there and fight!"

"Next up, numbers 93 and 94!" the ref called.

Here it comes, Krillin thought as he climbed onto the mat.

"Too bad you don't get a *real* opponent," the shorter fighter laughed.

"Well, at least I'll get to play with my little friend!" the taller one replied as he climbed onto the mat.

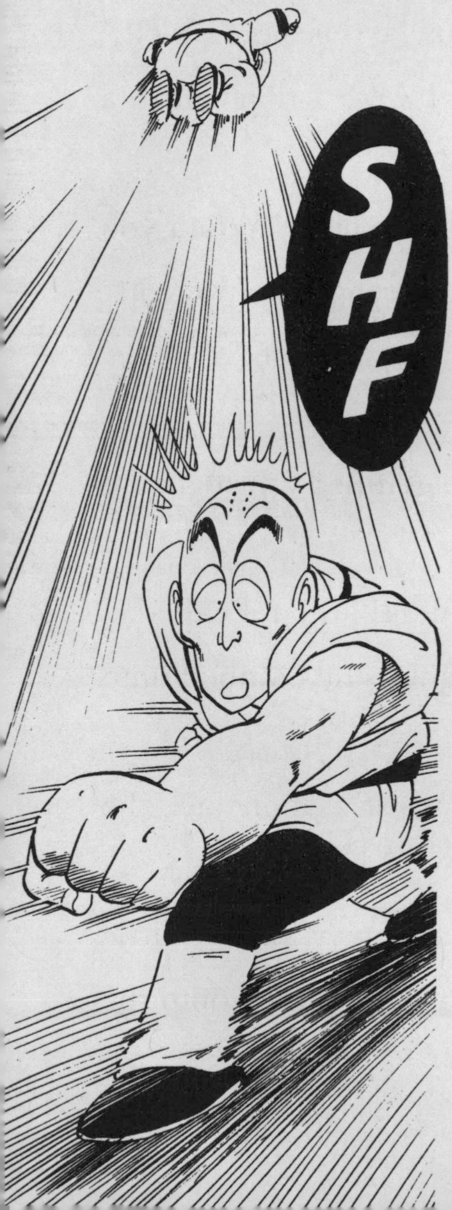
SHF

"Just remember what I told you!" Goku said. "Fight with everything you've got!"

"D-don't make fun of me!" Krillin whined.

The referee yelled, "Go!" And the bully lunged.

For a second, Krillin stood frozen with fear. Then he jumped. His powerful legs pushed him high into the air, and his opponent's fist struck at nothing.

Krillin landed lightly, then extended his leg and aimed a crushing kick at his opponent's gut. He kicked with all the strength he had.

Krillin's "friend" soared through the air and crashed

through the far wall of Competition Hall. Very, *very* out of bounds.

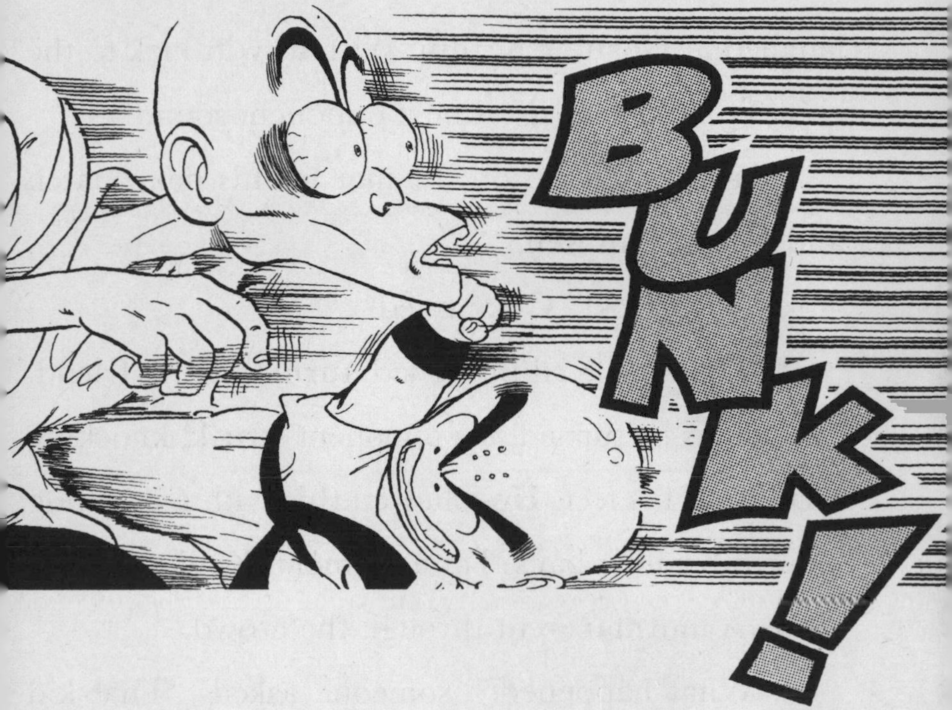
BUNK!

Everyone was stunned, including Goku. Finally the referee stammered, "V-v-victory! To n-n-number 93!"

"*Now* do you see?" Goku cheered. "Thanks to the old timer's training, we've gotten way stronger than we realized!"

Krillin looked down at his legs in amazement. "N-n-no fooling!" he grinned.

When the next round of fights started, no one laughed at Goku or Krillin. With a swift kick to the chin, Goku defeated his next opponent soundly.

Krillin climbed on the mat for his next match and steadied himself.

"Good luck!" Goku cried.

"Thanks!" Krillin replied, turning to his friend. As soon as he turned, his opponent struck, knocking Krillin off his feet. He followed this with a crushing blow to Krillin's back. For a moment, Krillin just lay there. A murmur went through the crowd.

"What happened?" someone asked. "That kid looked awesome a minute ago."

"Guess it was just a fluke," someone else replied.

Suddenly, Krillin popped up. "Betcha thought I was down for the count," he laughed. "Truth is, that didn't hurt at all!"

His opponent gaped. “Impossible!” he sputtered. “No one gets up after an attack from me!”

“Well,” Krillin smirked, “meet no one.”

The other fighter took one look at Krillin’s determined face and dashed behind the referee. “Mercy!” he cried. “Mercy! Mercy!”

The next rounds went even faster as Goku and Krillin took out one opponent after another. Finally, it was time for the match that would determine the first contestant from their block to fight in the finals. Goku’s opponent was not huge or especially muscular, but he was very quick and very skilled.

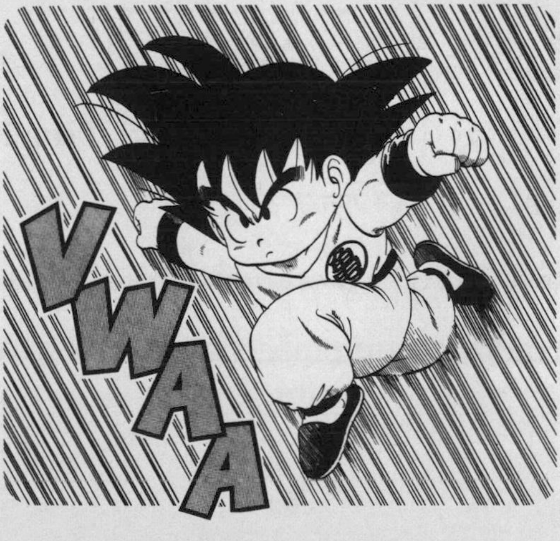
VWAA

"You better qualify, Goku!" Krillin yelled with a huge grin on his face. "I don't wanna enter this contest without you!"

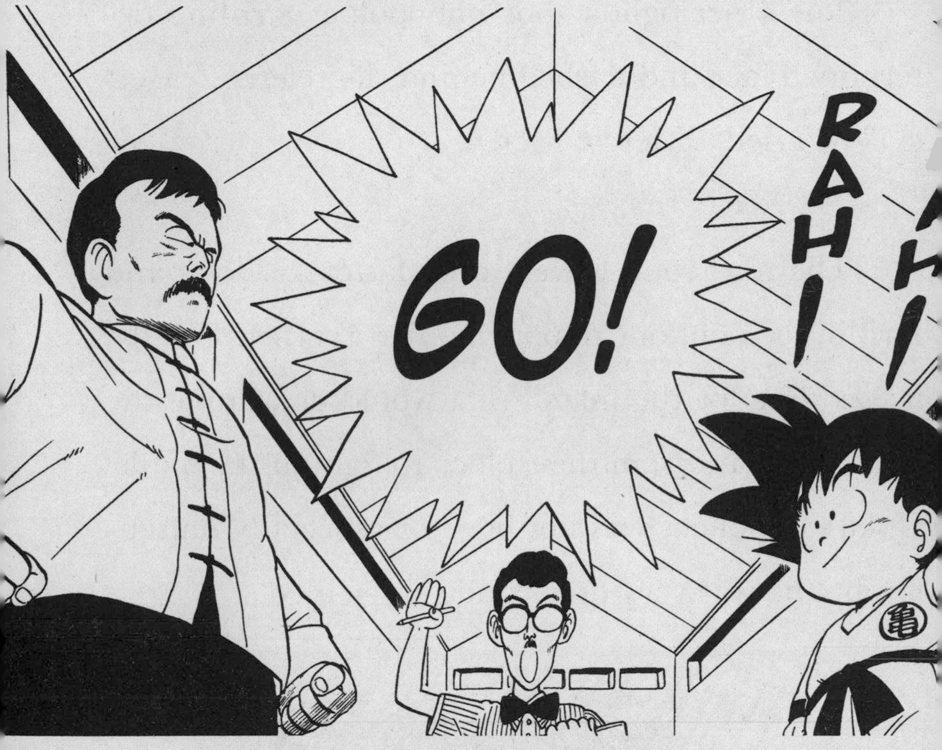
GO!
RAH!
AH!

"Go!" yelled the referee, and Goku struck a combat pose.

"What a wretched stance, child!" his opponent scoffed. "You're completely vulnerable to my Lion-Fang Fu!"

He swung at Goku—but Goku wasn't there.

"Yoo-hoo!" called Goku from above.

"You're fast," the man hissed. "Almost as fast... as *me*!"

As Goku dropped toward him, the man cartwheeled out of the way. He whipped around and brought his hand up like a snake ready to strike. But Goku kicked his legs out from under him.

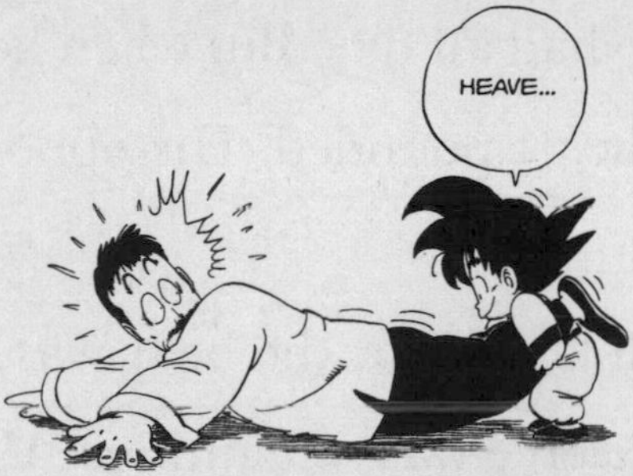
HEAVE...

The man dropped to the mat. Goku grabbed his legs and heaved him out of the ring.

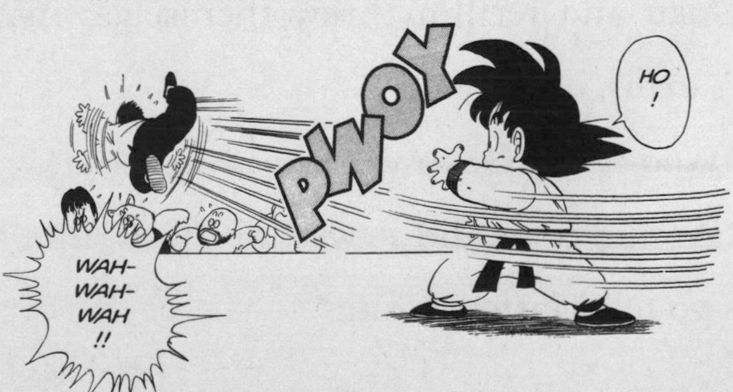
HO
!
PWOY
WAH-
WAH-
WAH
!!

"Out of bounds!" said the referee. "Number 70 goes to the finals!"

"Woo-hoo!" yelled Goku.

"You *did* it, Goku!" laughed Krillin, hugging him. "You really *did* it!"

"Now," the referee said, "the final contestants for Block 3 will enter the ring!"

"My turn!" yelled Krillin, sounding more confident than he had all day. But when he stepped onto the mat, his heart pounded. His opponent was a giant bear.

One high kick later, the bear was rolling off the mat and the referee was screaming, "Victory to Krillin! He joins the Final Eight in the Strongest Under the Heavens Tournament!"

Goku and Krillin threw themselves into each other's arms.

"Woo-hoo!" Goku yelled.

"We did it we did it we did it!" Krillin yelled. "Let's go tell Master Roshi!"

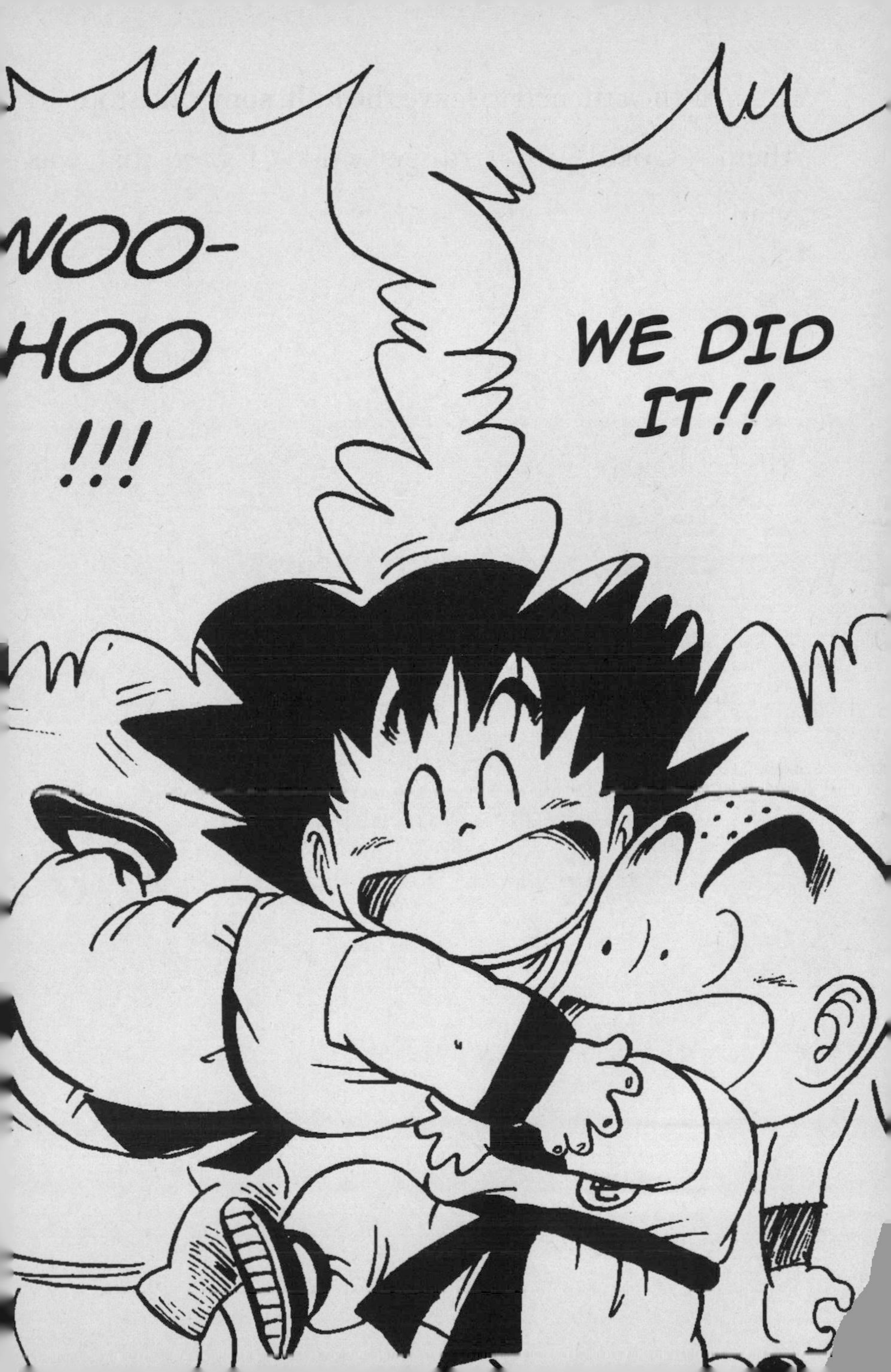
WE DID IT!!
NOO-HOO !!!

As they turned to leave the hall, someone stopped them. "Goku!" the stranger said. "I *knew* that was you!"

Chapter Four

"Huh?" Goku said, staring at the man. "Who are you?"

"Don't tell me you've forgotten," the man said. Then he struck a martial-arts pose and shouted, "Fist of the wolf fang!"

"Yamcha!" cried Goku, finally recognizing his old friend. "Wow! Long time no see! Your hair's all different. Where did it go?"

Yamcha sighed. "Well, Bulma made me cut it. She said it made me look like a crazy desert bandit."

"But you *are* a crazy desert bandit!" Goku laughed.

"B-b-bandit?!" Krillin gulped.

Goku introduced Krillin to Yamcha then told him the whole story. He talked about looking for the Dragon Balls with his friends Bulma and Oolong. About how Yamcha and his cat Pu'ar had tried to steal the balls but then became their friends. And about how Yamcha had once been terrified of girls until he fell in love with Bulma.

"And now you're a contestant?" Krillin asked Yamcha.

"I just won my qualifying round!" Yamcha replied proudly. "I'm one of the eight finalists!"

"All right!" Goku said. "Maybe you and I will get to fight again!"

"I'm afraid I wouldn't have a chance against

you," Yamcha smiled. "Master Roshi's training has put you on a whole other level."

"Yeah, I'm pretty surprised how strong I got!" Goku said. "Krillin too!"

"*Both* of you trained with Master Roshi?" Yamcha sighed. "Suddenly even second place isn't looking very likely.

"Hey, I almost forgot!" he said, brightening. "Bulma, Pu'ar, and Oolong are here too!"

"Really?" Goku said happily. "Come on, Krillin! I want you to meet my friends!"

Goku raced outside with Krillin close behind. They pushed through the crowd, but they couldn't see a thing from where they stood. Goku looked up and saw a man whose head was just the right size and shape for a perch. A moment later, he was standing on top of the man's head, scanning the crowd.

"There they are!" Goku cried. "And they're with the Turtle Guy!"

Master Roshi was extremely happy to see Bulma.

"My, my, how have you been?" he asked.

"Just fine," she replied. "Where are you living now? I went to your island to visit Goku, but there's nothing there!"

"That place was too small for serious training, so we moved to a much bigger island. But never mind that," the old master smiled. "Are you still with Yamcha?"

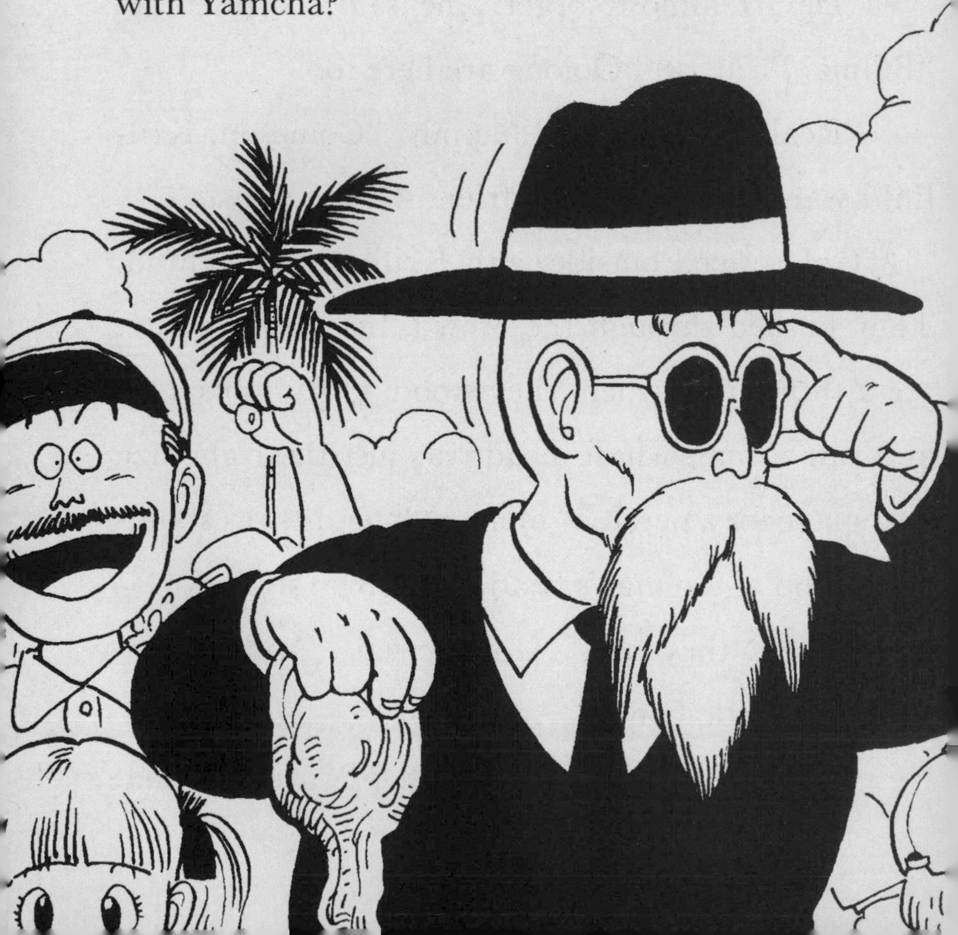

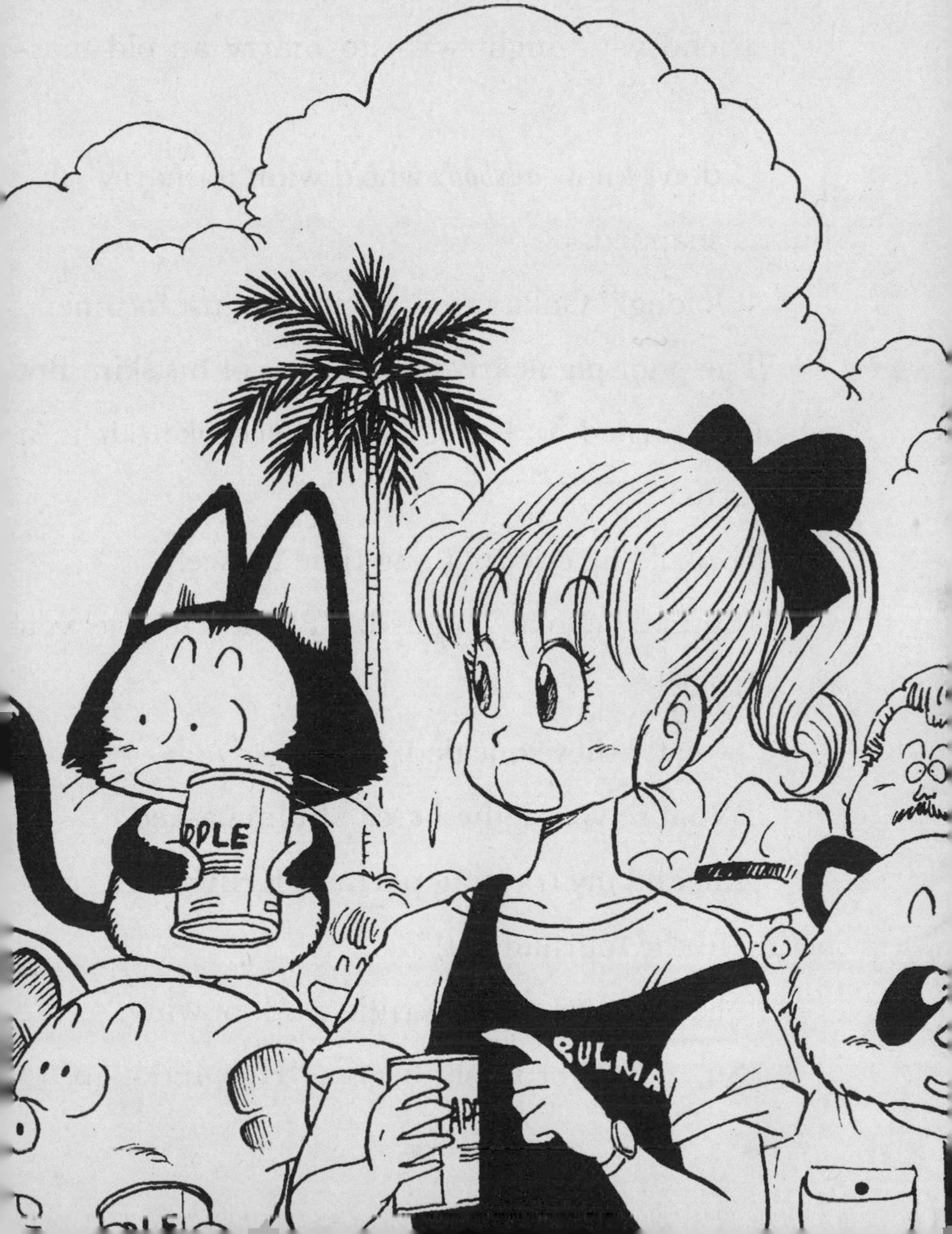
BULMA

"Yes," Bulma replied, giving him a sideways look.

"What a shame. Any chance you've got a sister or a friend who might want to marry an old master…"

"I don't know *anybody* who'd want to marry *you*," Bulma snapped.

"Oolong!" Goku cried, racing up just in time.

The poor pig nearly jumped out of his skin. But when he turned and saw Goku, he broke out in a huge grin.

"Goku!" he cried. "Long time no see!"

"Bulma!" Goku laughed. "Pu'ar! How've you guys been?!"

"Great!" they squealed.

"What're you doing here?" Bulma asked.

"Me and my training partner, Krillin, are competing in the tournament!"

"Nice to meet you," Krillin said, bowing.

"So…" Master Roshi began. "How did it go?"

Goku and Krillin just looked at each other and laughed.

"Get out!" Bulma gasped. "You actually did it?"

"And Yamcha too!" Goku grinned.

"Huzzah!" Bulma cried.

"Count on Goku," Oolong chuckled.

"Nice job," smiled the master. "Nice job indeed."

In the midst of all the cheering and laughing came an announcement from the loudspeaker: "The Strongest Under the Heavens Tournament will begin momentarily! Will the eight finalists please assemble in the main martial arts hall?"

"Sounds like they want you guys," Bulma said.

"All right then," Goku said as he scrambled over the wall of the hall. "See you later."

Krillin followed him up and over.

"Good luck!" the others all yelled.

Bulma shook her head and smiled. "He's still

such a little kid!"

"Hey," Oolong said, looking around. "Where's the old guy?"

"What are you talking about?" snapped Bulma. "He's...hey! Master Roshi's *gone*!"

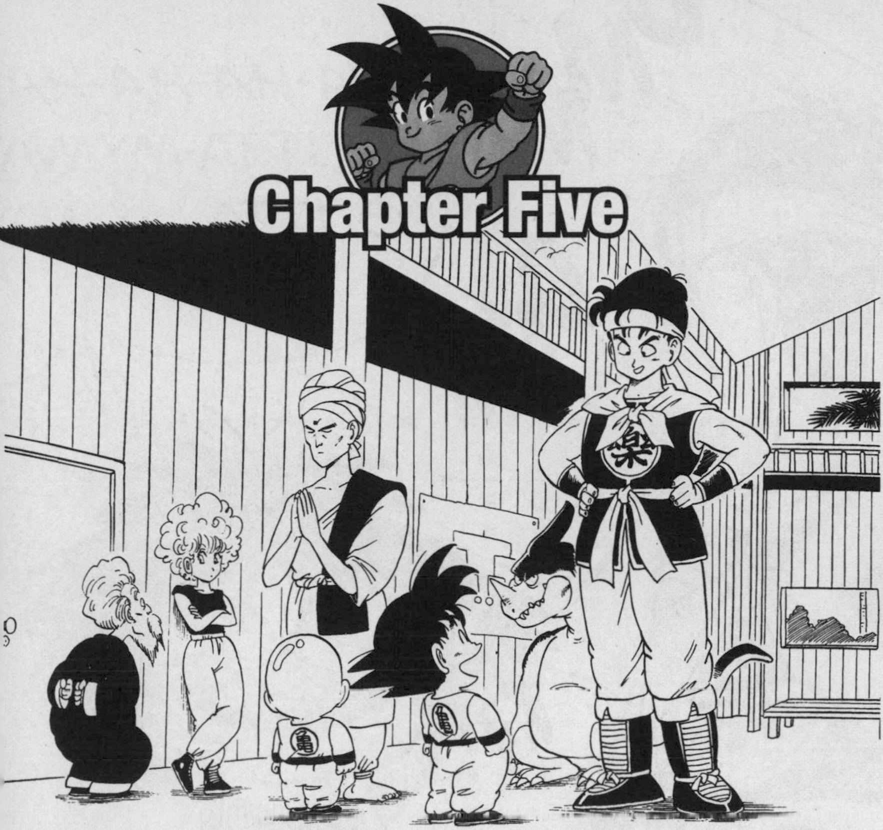

Chapter Five

Goku and Krillin raced back to the main hall where Yamcha and the other contestants were waiting. There was a tall, quiet man who looked incredibly focused, a flying dinosaur, a pretty young woman with curly hair, and an old man with a beard.

"There's only seven of us," Goku said. "I thought there were–"

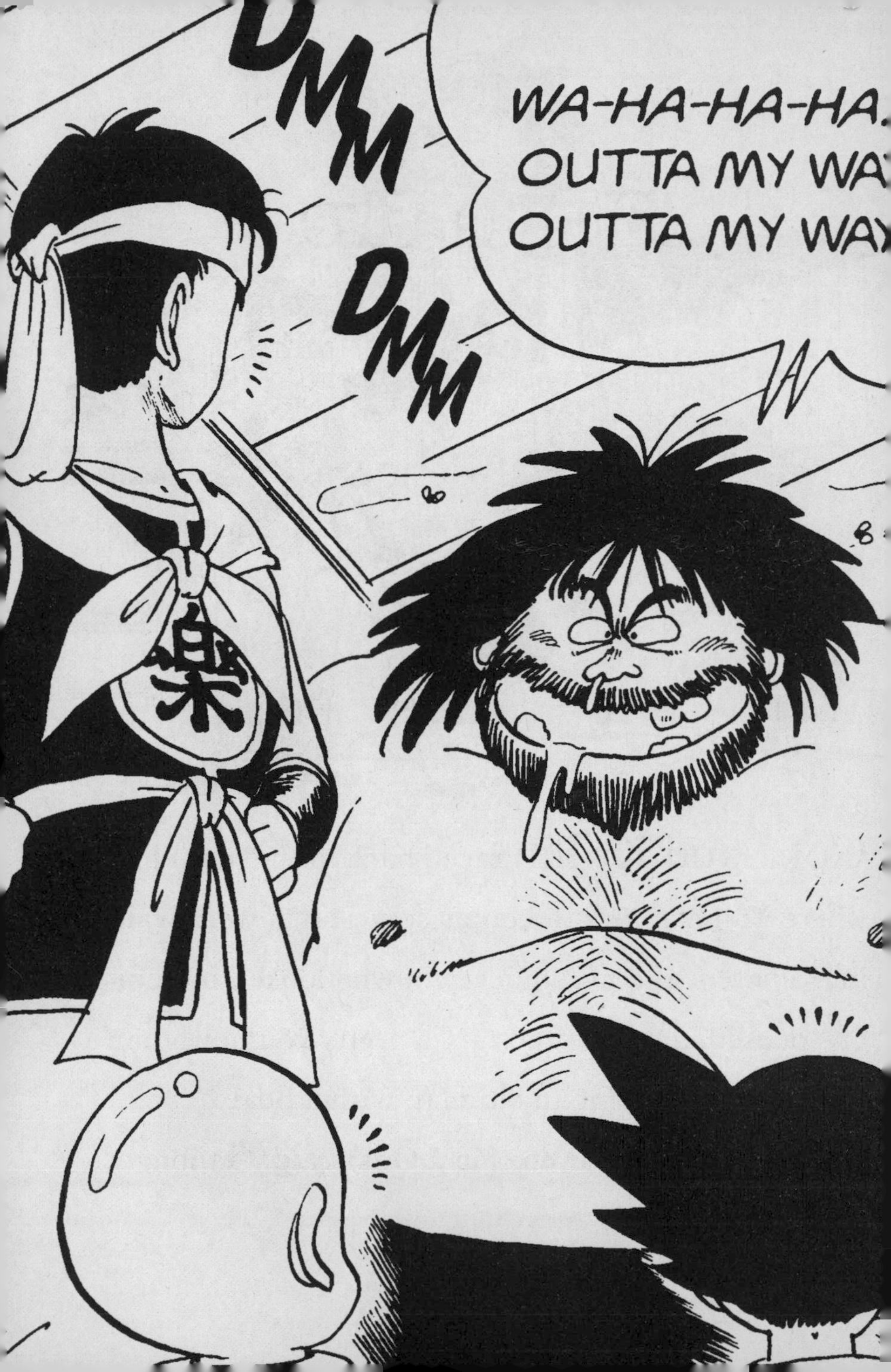
WA-HA-HA-HA.
OUTTA MY WA
OUTTA MY WA
DMM
DMM

"Outta my way!" someone boomed. "Outta my way!"

Goku turned. Coming toward him was a big, sweaty beast of a man with a shock of unruly hair. Flies buzzed around his head. Food-specked drool slopped from his mouth. Snot oozed through the crust in his nose.

Then Goku caught a whiff of him. The smell brought tears to his eyes.

"It hurts!" he cried. "My nose is sharp as a dog's! That stench is killing me!"

"Wh-who is that?" Krillin asked.

Yamcha held his nose. "That's Bacterian!" he said. "His strength is legendary, but his smell is his not-so-secret weapon. He hasn't taken a bath in his *entire life*!"

Krillin gasped.

"When they get a whiff of his terrible stench," Yamcha continued, "his opponents instinctively hold their noses. When they only have one hand to fight with—he strikes!"

"Stink-Fu!" Krillin cried.

Just then the tournament announcer stepped into the room. "Now hear this!" he called. "All finalists please assemble here and—"

Suddenly hit by a wall of Bacterian's funk, he retched. "Everyone except you," he gasped, bringing a hanky to his nose. "You—you can feel free to take a few steps back."

When Bacterian was at a manageable distance, the announcer continued. "We will now determine the match-ups. When your name is called, please—"

The old man with the beard wasn't paying attention.

"—Sir?" the announcer called to him. But the old man had other things on his mind.

"You wouldn't happen to be married, would you?" he asked the pretty young woman with the curly hair.

"*Sir*!!" the announcer yelled.

The old man turned and looked at him innocently. "Yes?"

"Okay," the announcer said, clearing his throat. "When your name is called, please come here and draw a slip of paper." He looked at the clipboard in his hand. "First up, Namu."

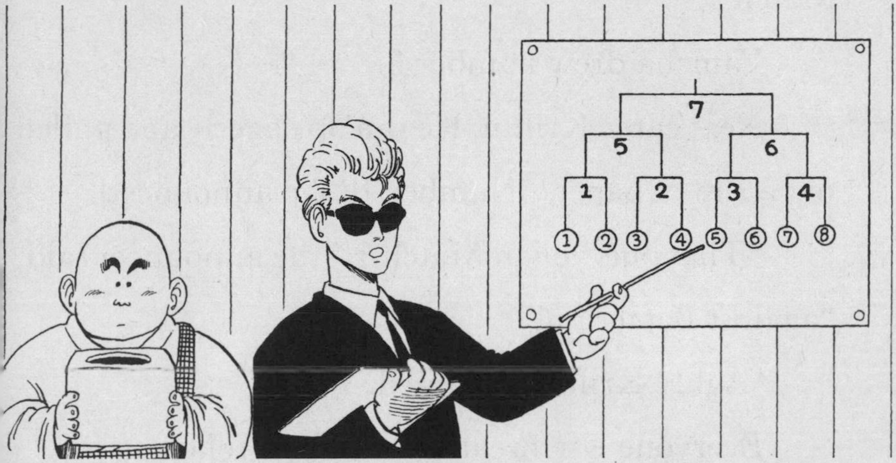
7
5
6
1
2
3
4
①
②
③
④
⑤
⑥
⑦
⑧

"That is I," said the tall, quiet man. He drew a slip of paper from the box the announcer was holding. "Number 6," he said.

"You'll be in Match 3," the announcer said, writing Namu's name on a big chart on the wall. "Next is...Giran."

"Yo!" sneered the winged dinosaur. He pulled number 8 out of the box, which meant he would fight in Match 4.

The announcer pinched his nose more tightly with his hanky and called, "Bacterian!" The fetid fighter drew number 2, which meant he would fight in Match 1.

Yamcha drew number 3.

Next came Krillin. He ran up eagerly and pulled out a slip of paper. "Number 1!" he announced.

"That puts you in Match 1," the announcer said, "against Bacterian!"

"Agh!" Krillin screamed.

Everyone else breathed a sigh of relief.

"Song Oku!" the announcer cried. "Please come up and take your number."

When no one approached, the announcer tried again. "Are you here, Song Oku?"

Still no one responded.

"That's funny. We have the right number of

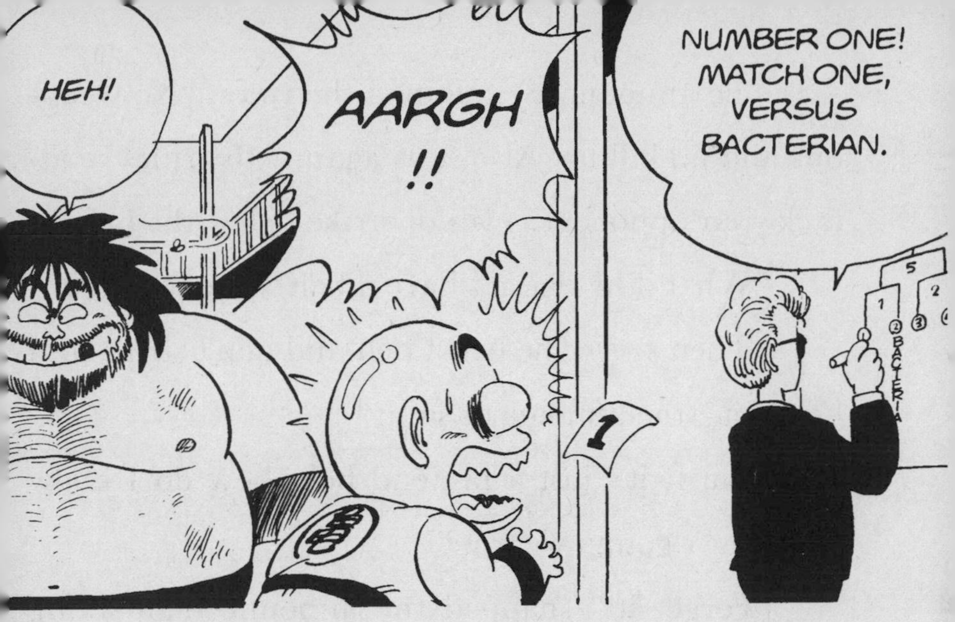
NUMBER ONE! MATCH ONE, VERSUS BACTERIAN.
BACTERIA
AARGH!!
HEH!

people here…" the announcer mused.

"Do you mean Son Goku?" Yamcha asked, looking at the paper in the announcer's hand.

"Er–Son Goku? Is there a Son Goku here?" the announcer asked.

"Here!" Goku called, raising both arms. He drew number 7, which meant he would fight Giran.

Ran Fuan, the woman with the curly hair, was matched against the quiet Namu. Jackie Chun, the old man with the beard, would challenge Yamcha in Match 2.

The announcer explained the rules: "No weapons and no killing. Also, it is against the rules to attack your opponent's eyes or strike below the belt."

"What if he doesn't have a belt?" Goku asked.

"Then *pretend* he has a belt and don't strike him below it," the announcer said.

"But if it's just a pretend belt, how do I know where he's gonna wear it?"

"Forget it!" snapped the announcer, breaking out in a sweat. "Just…try not to break the rules!" He took a few deep breaths and wiped his face with his hanky. "The matches will begin in—"

"When do we get lunch?" Goku asked, tugging on the announcer's sleeve.

"What?!" the announcer barked. "No one eats right before a match!"

"I wanna eat!" Goku moaned.

And so they waited while Goku had seconds and thirds.

Finally, the announcer's voice filled the arena:

"Ladies and gentlemen, we thank you for your patience! The Strongest Under the Heavens Tournament now begins!"

THE BATTLES ARE ABOUT TO BEGIN!!!

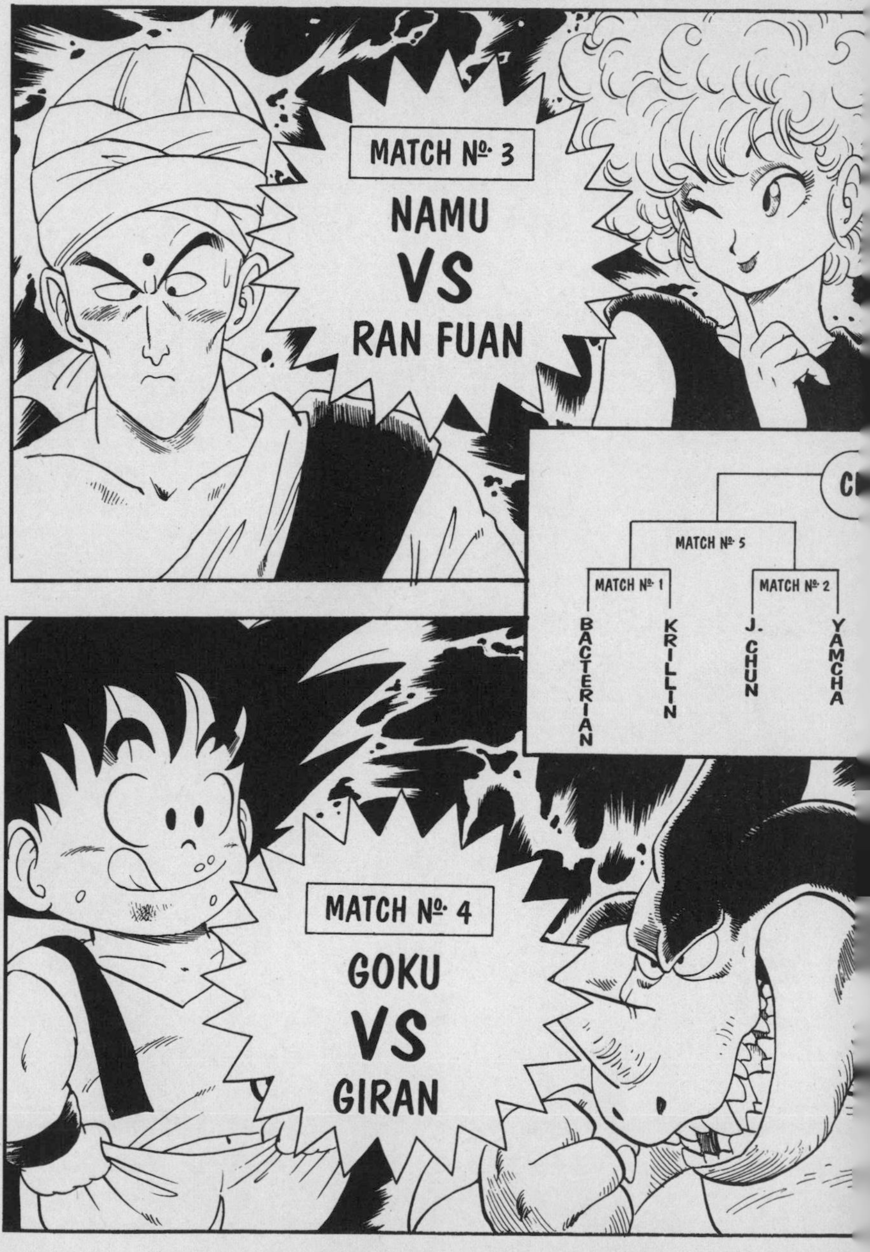
MATCH Nº 3
NAMU
VS
RAN FUAN
MATCH Nº 5
MATCH Nº 2
MATCH Nº 1
YAMCHA
J. CHUN
KRILLIN
BACTERIAN
MATCH Nº 4
GOKU
VS
GIRAN

ALL HAIL OUR 8 TENKA'ICHI BUDŌKAI CHALLENGERS!!!

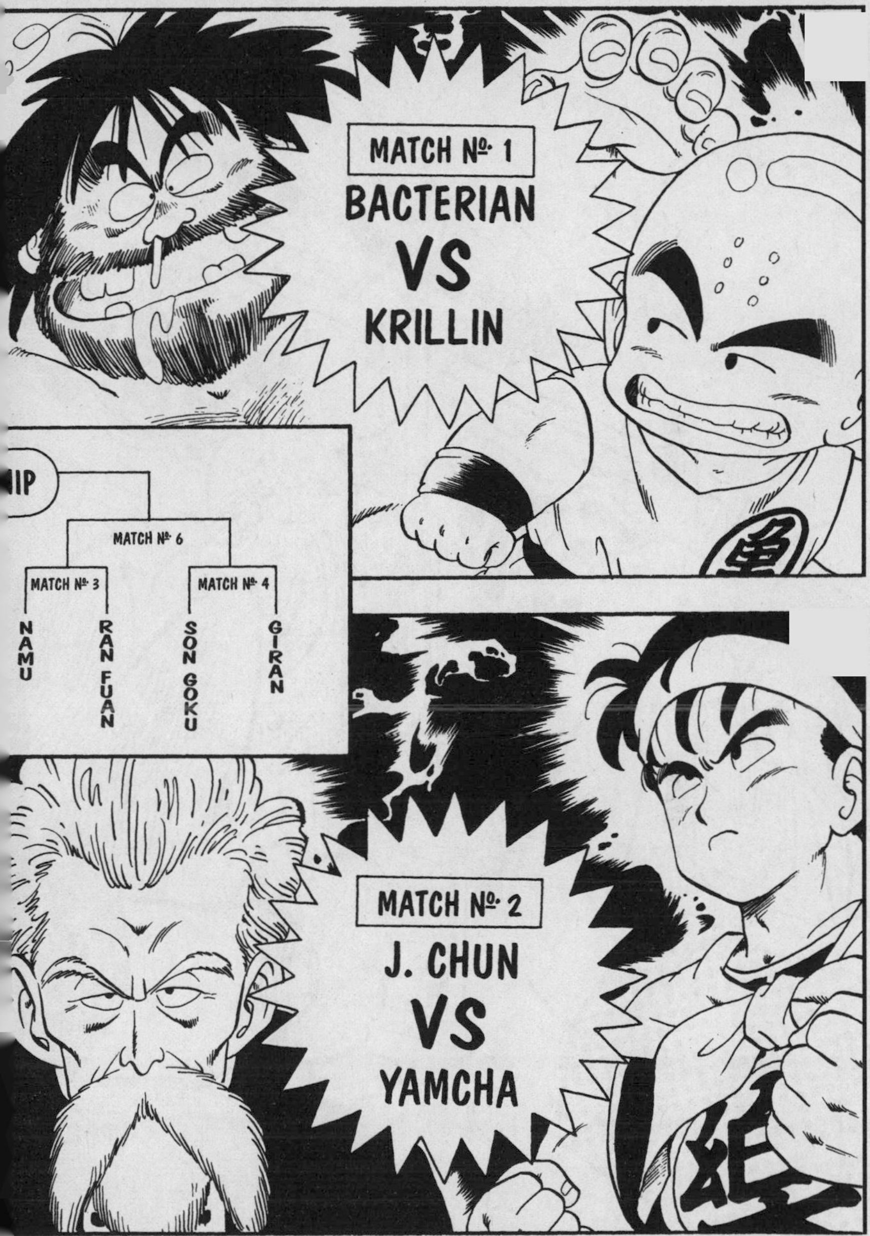
MATCH Nº 1
BACTERIAN
VS
KRILLIN
IP
MATCH Nº 6
MATCH Nº 3
MATCH Nº 4
NAMU
RAN FUAN
SON GOKU
GIRAN
MATCH Nº 2
J. CHUN
VS
YAMCHA

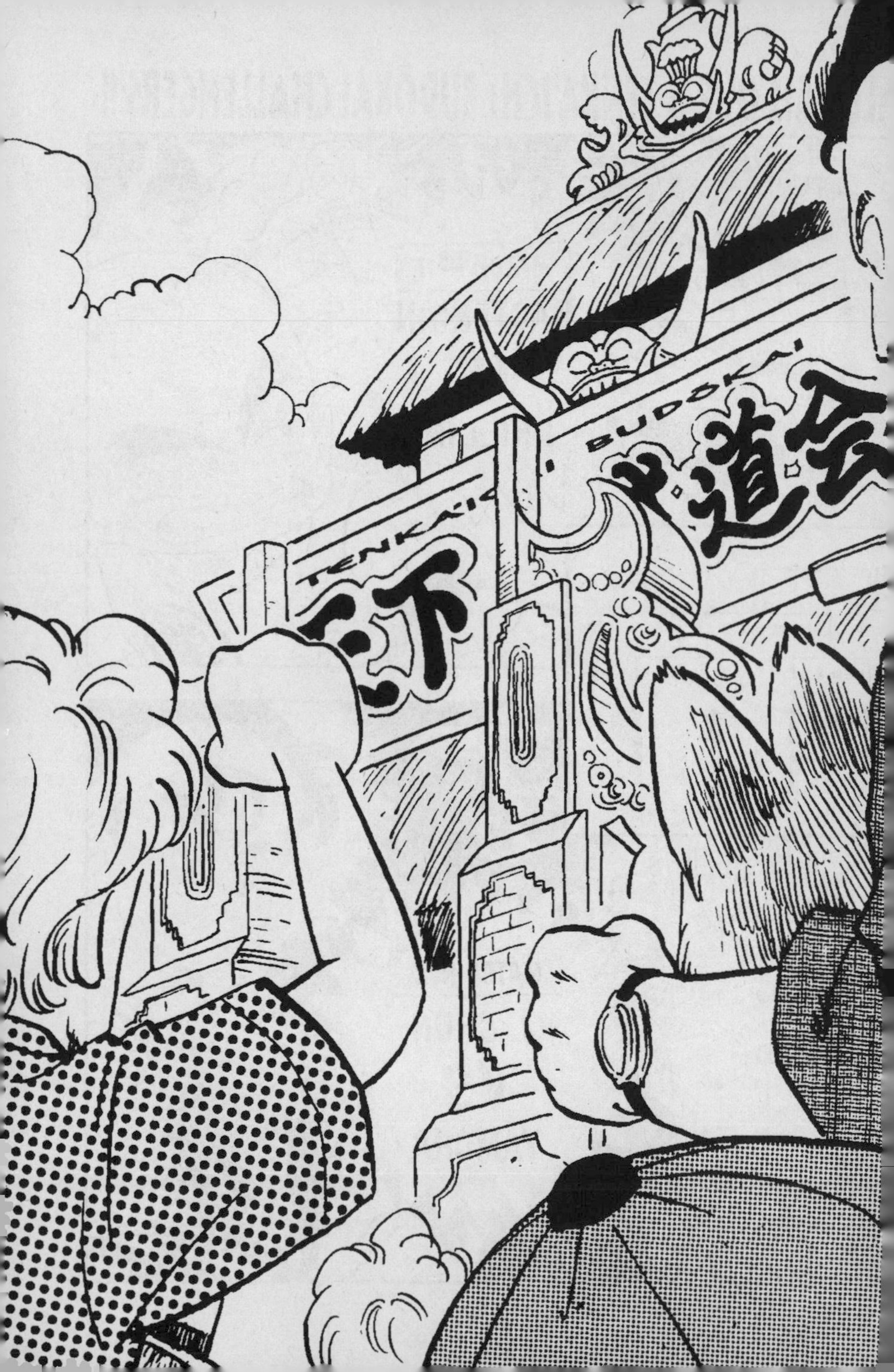

BUDŌKAI
下
道

Chapter Six

The crowd cheered so loudly that it was almost impossible to hear the next announcement: "Remember," the announcer boomed, "the winner of this tournament will be awarded 500,000 Zeni in prize money!

"But before the match begins, let's have a word of wisdom from our resident wise man."

A weary-looking hound stepped close to the announcer.

"Venerable master, if you please," the announcer said, handing the dog the microphone.

The dog waited patiently for the crowd to settle. When everyone was quiet, the dog took a deep breath. Everyone waited anxiously for the very wise and knowing thing he was about to say:

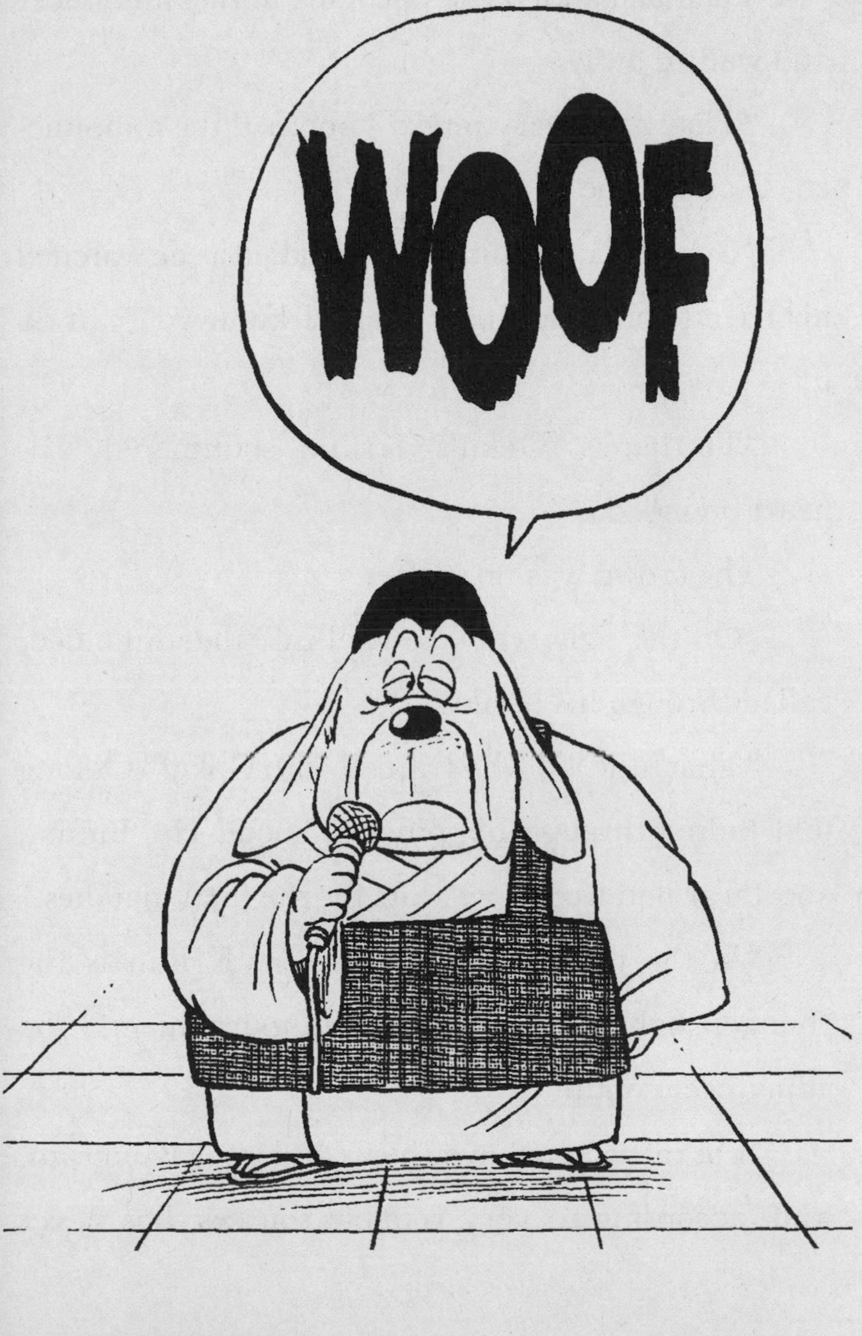
WOOF

Then he handed the mic back to the announcer and walked away.

"Thank you very much!" boomed the announcer. "Now, let the games begin!"

"Good luck, Krillin!" Goku called as he watched his friend enter the finals ring. "I know you can do it!"

"Th-thanks, Goku!" Krillin stammered. His heart pounded.

The crowd was on its feet.

"On the right we have Krillin!" the announcer called through his hanky.

"That's the kid who trained with Goku!" Oolong told Bulma through his pinched snout. He, Bulma, and Pu'ar had front-row seats for the final matches.

"At the tender age of thirteen, Krillin is the youngest fighter ever to enter the tournament!" the announcer continued.

"On the left we have the malodorous Bacterian, who, according to very reliable sources, has never taken a bath in his life!"

"But where is Master Roshi?!" Bulma snapped. "This is his own students' match!"

"Remember, contestants," the announcer went on, "if you fall off this stage, beg for mercy, or are knocked down for ten seconds or more, you lose! But in the finals, there is *no* time limit!"

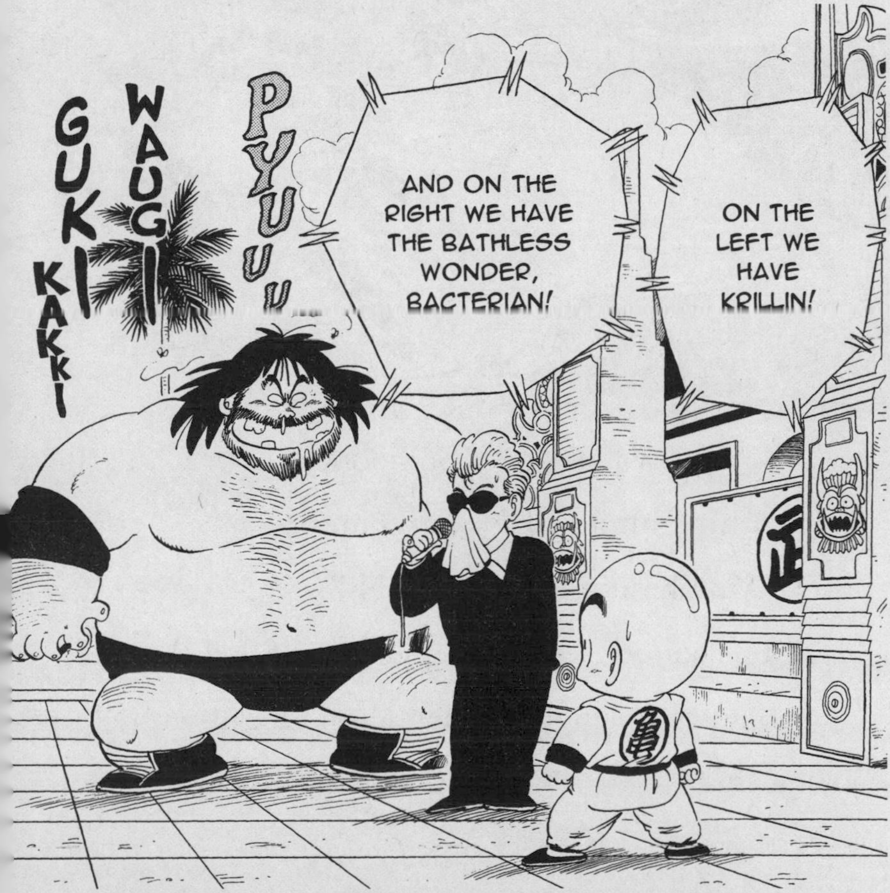
ON THE LEFT WE HAVE KRILLIN!
AND ON THE RIGHT WE HAVE THE BATHLESS WONDER, BACTERIAN!
PYUUU
WAUGI
GUKI
KAKKI

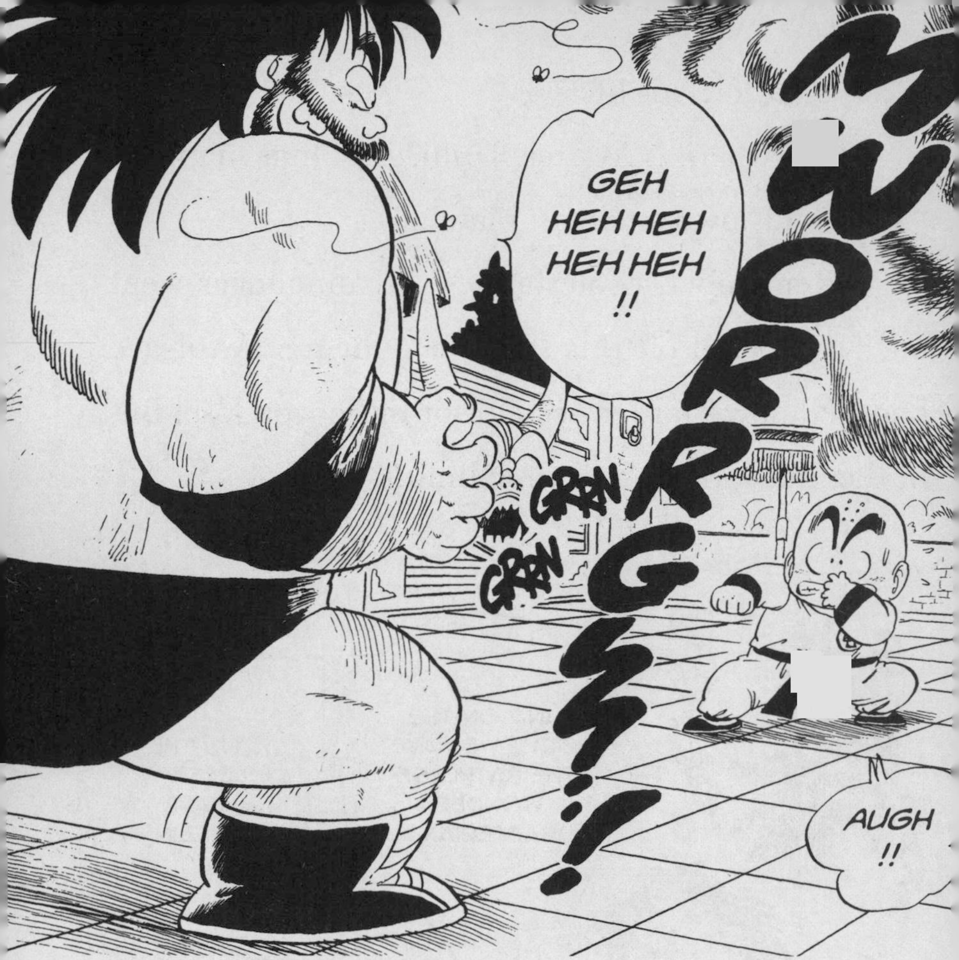
GEH HEH HEH HEH HEH !!
GRRN
GRRN
AUGH !!

The crowd groaned. Someone cried, "Can't they have a time limit just for *this* match?"

"Match number 1, BEGIN!"

The sound of gongs and drums filled the air.

Bacterian laughed–then let out a gut-wrenching belch that threw a wave of stench at Krillin so powerful it almost knocked him down. Bacterian lunged at him, but Krillin was too fast. He jumped into the air and out of the way.

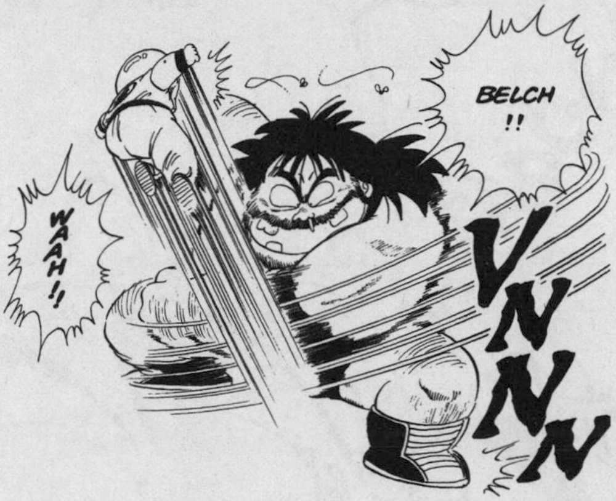
BELCH !!
WAAH!!
VNNN

"Nicely dodged, impudent brat," Bacterian said. Then he gave an evil laugh. "Now, try smelling my breath!"

Bacterian inhaled deeply–then exhaled a great cloud of green gas right in Krillin's face.

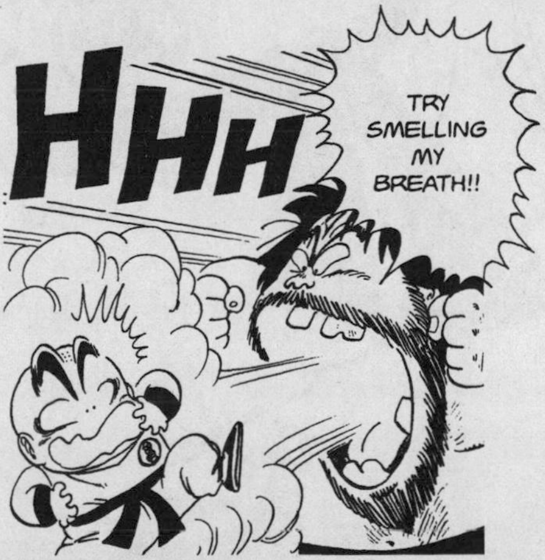
TRY SMELLING MY BREATH!!
HHH

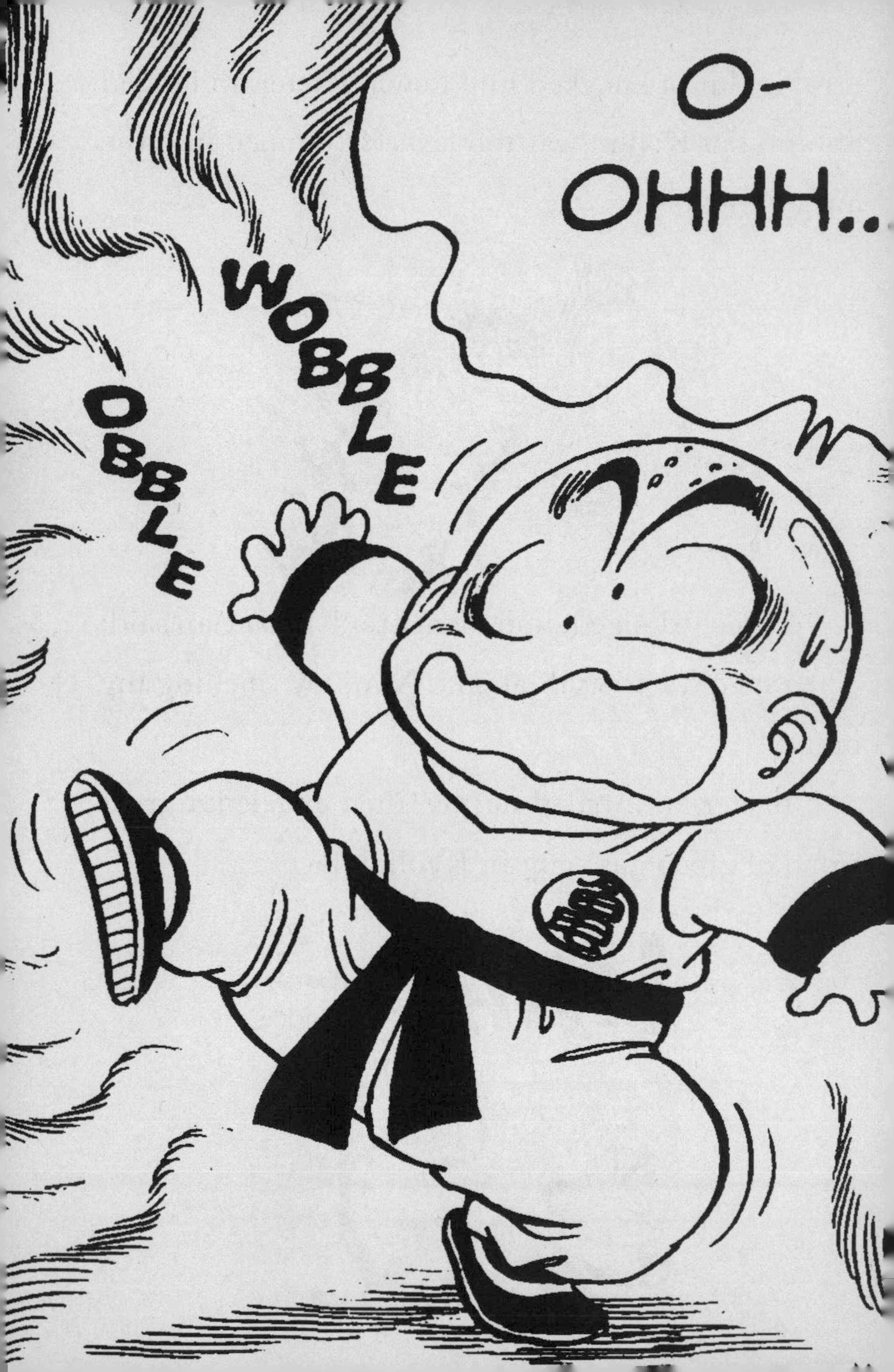
O-
OHHH...
WOBBLE
OBBLE

Krillin's eyes crossed and watered. He staggered backward and seemed unable to stand up straight.

"And now, while we're at it..." Bacterian chuckled. He reached his sweaty fingers into his armpit and dug deep. He scraped and scraped until his fingers were coated with a goo that bore a striking resemblance to hot melted cheese. Then–"Take that!" –he flung the stuff at Krillin.

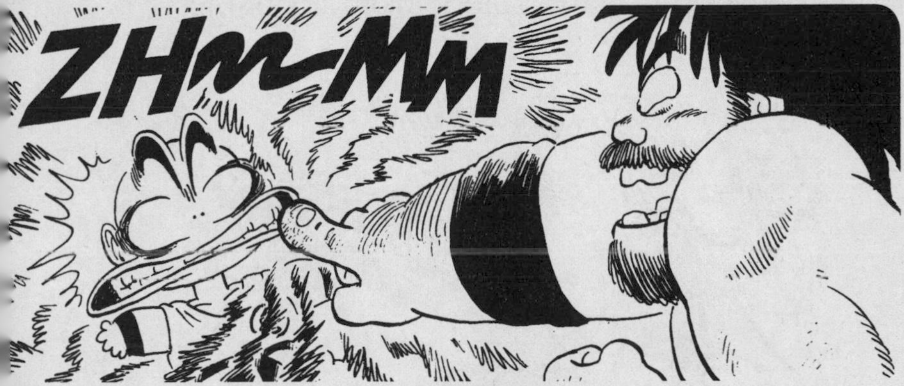
ZHM-MM

Krillin was no match for Bacterian's armpit assault. He fainted dead away.

"Krillin!" Goku yelled. "Get up, Krillin!"

"Krillin is down!" cried the announcer, who, along with several others in the arena, was now wearing a gas mask. "Bacterian's legendary breath-armpit combo was too much for him!"

The referee started the count.

But Bacterian wasn't finished. He walked over to the fallen Krillin, snot slithering from his nose, mixing with the drool leaking from his mouth. He squatted low, shook himself just a bit, and let the most horrible sound imaginable–no, no, even more horrible than that–explode from his pants.

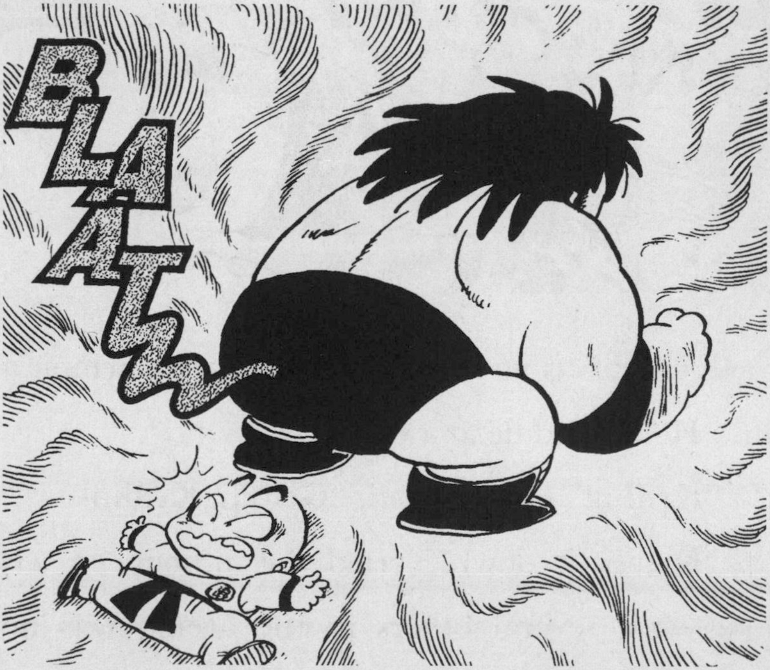
BLAAT

And then came the smell. The *smell*! Like a solid wall of foul. A soup of stench that would've shamed a surfeit of rotten egg-eating skunks on a hot day. It rolled over Krillin, then reached out for the crowd.

Some people fainted. Those strong enough to stay on their feet ran for the exits. Goku squeezed his nose with both hands and held his breath as tears streamed down his face.

"It's-it's the triple trump!" the announcer called through his mask. "Krillin is paralyzed! Helpless! There's no way he can recover from that!"

"Three! Four!" the referee called.

"Get up!" Goku called. "You can't lose to that big stinker! Hold your nose and..." A thought more powerful than Bacterian's putridity suddenly struck him.

"Five! Six!"

"Krillin!" Goku yelled, suddenly excited. "The smell! It's all in your head!"

"Seven!"' counted the referee.

"There's no way you can smell any of this!" Goku yelled.

"Eight!" counted the referee.

"Krillin!!" Goku screamed. "You haven't got a NOSE!"

Krillin's eyes fluttered open. "Huh?" he said.

"Nine!" counted the referee.

"W…wait a minute," Krillin said. "You're right! I haven't got a *nose!*"

The referee's mouth was forming the word "ten" when Krillin jumped to his feet.

Chapter Seven

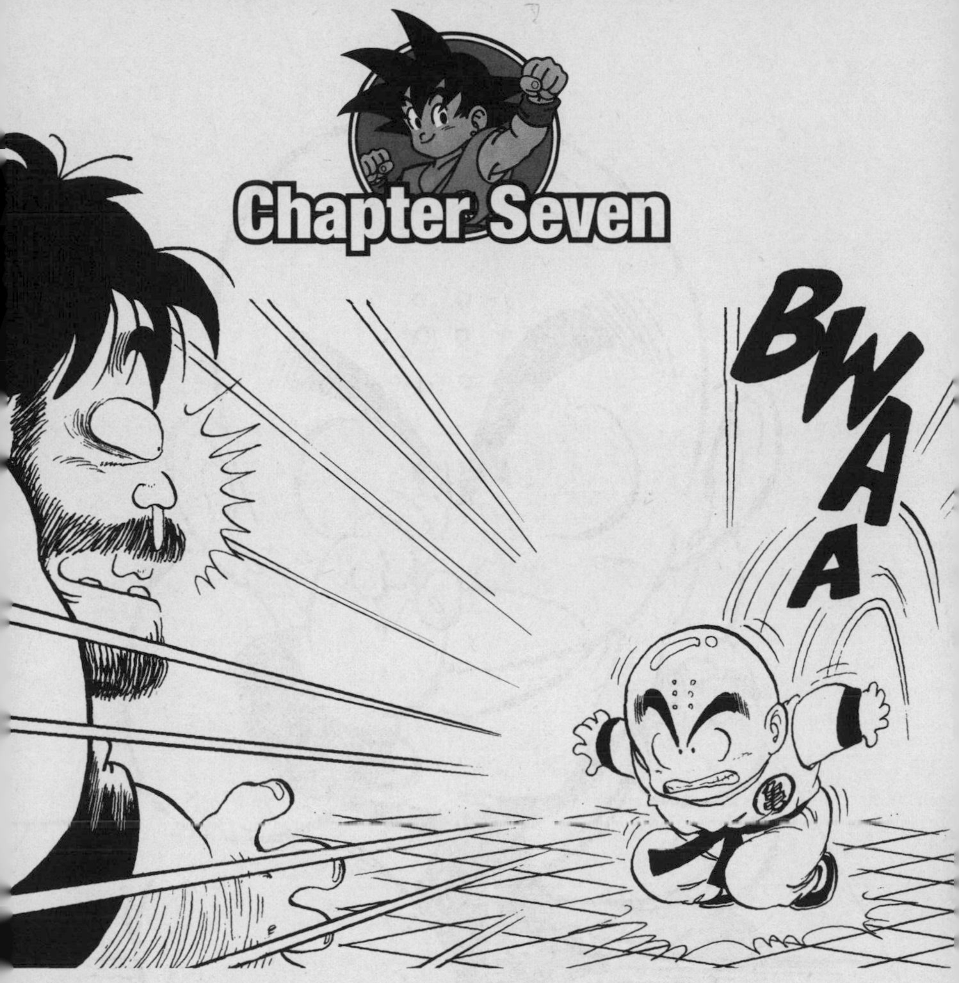
BWAA

The crowd roared, and Goku cheered loudest of all.

"It's incredible!" the announcer yelled. "The match is still on!"

Bacterian was so shocked his snot missed a drip.

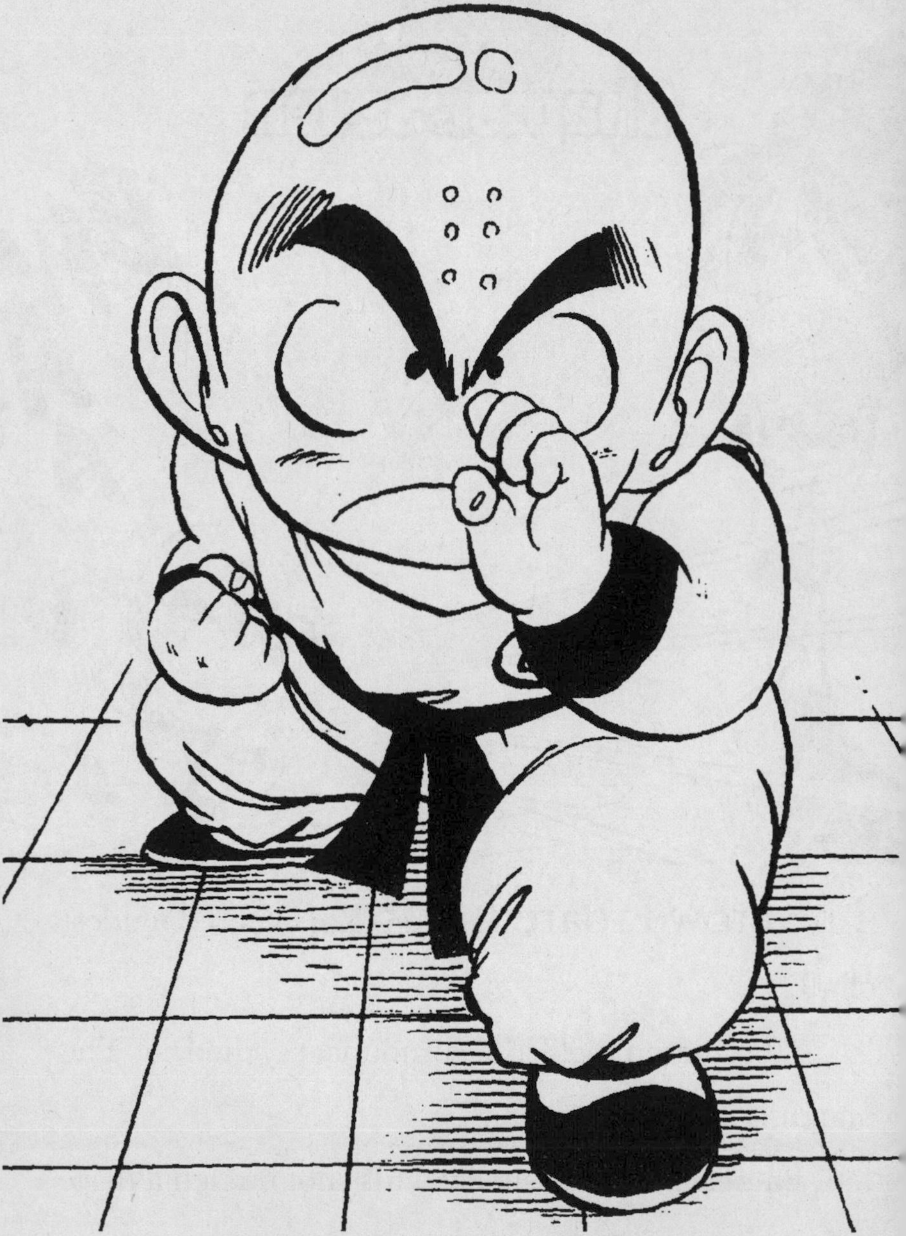

"No nose? It's not fair!"

"Okay, stinkpot!" Krillin said, striking a fighting stance. "HERE I COME!"

"Fortunately," Bacterian laughed, "I know more than Stink-Fu!" He made a series of scratching and snorting sounds deep in his throat. Then he summoned up a hot mouthful of congestion and gave it a swish.

MWORSH

MWORSH...

"He's about to use Phlegm-Fu!" the announcer yelled. "Will Krillin be able to survive the legendary loogies from which even elephants run in fear?"

When his cheeks were nearly bursting with the stuff, he spat it out at Krillin in short, quick bursts.

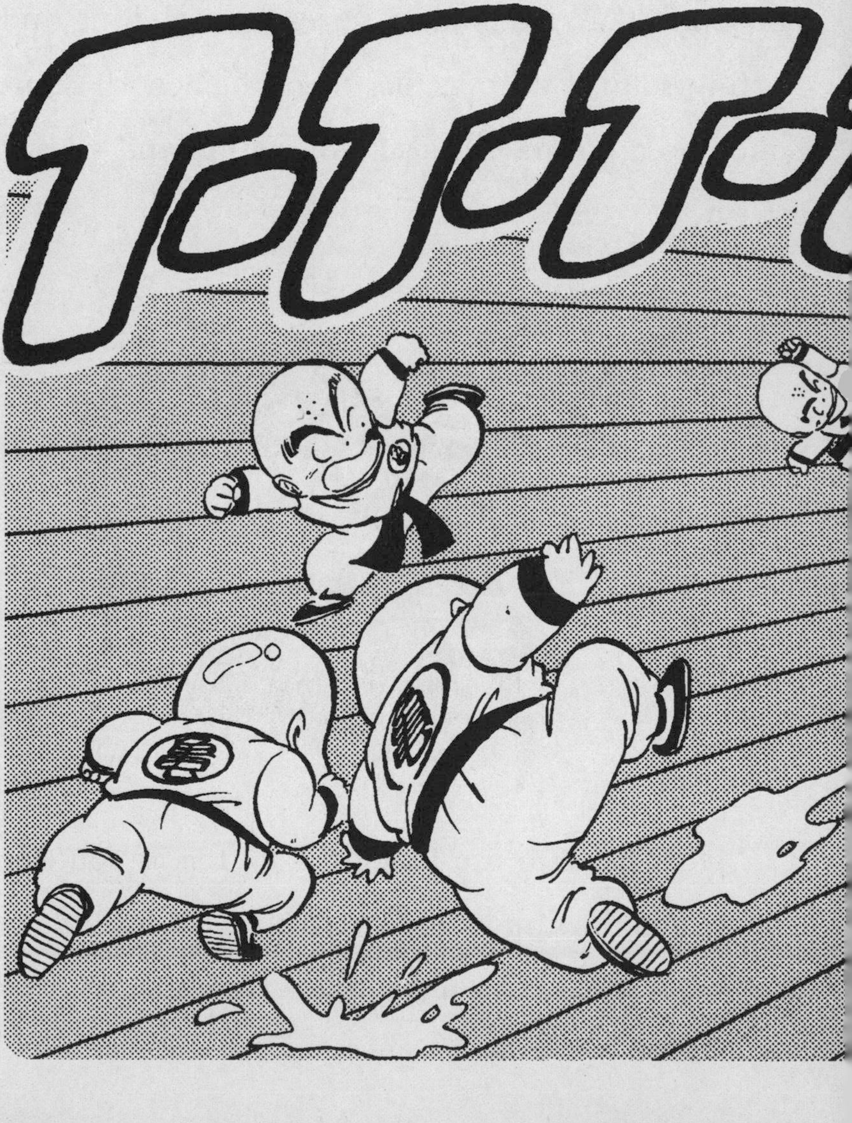

Krillin dodged the mucus missiles, steadied himself, and leapt into the air, his foot aimed at Bacterian's face.

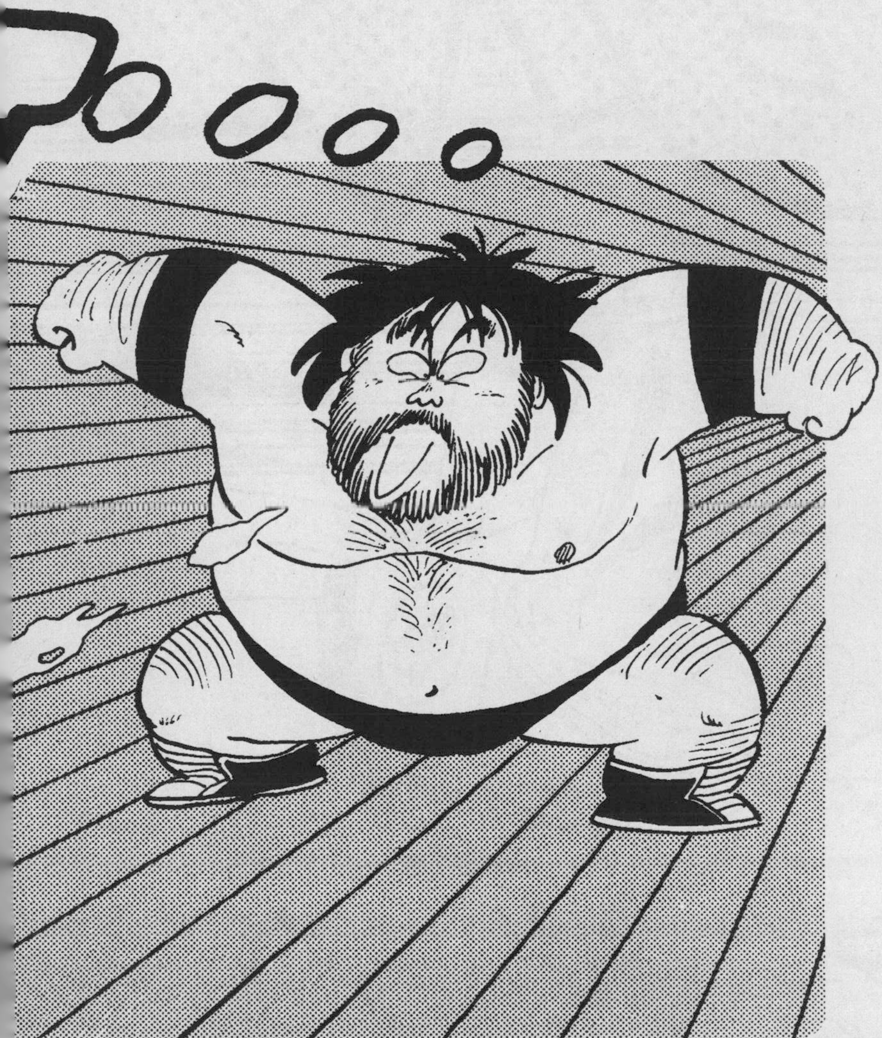
Poooo

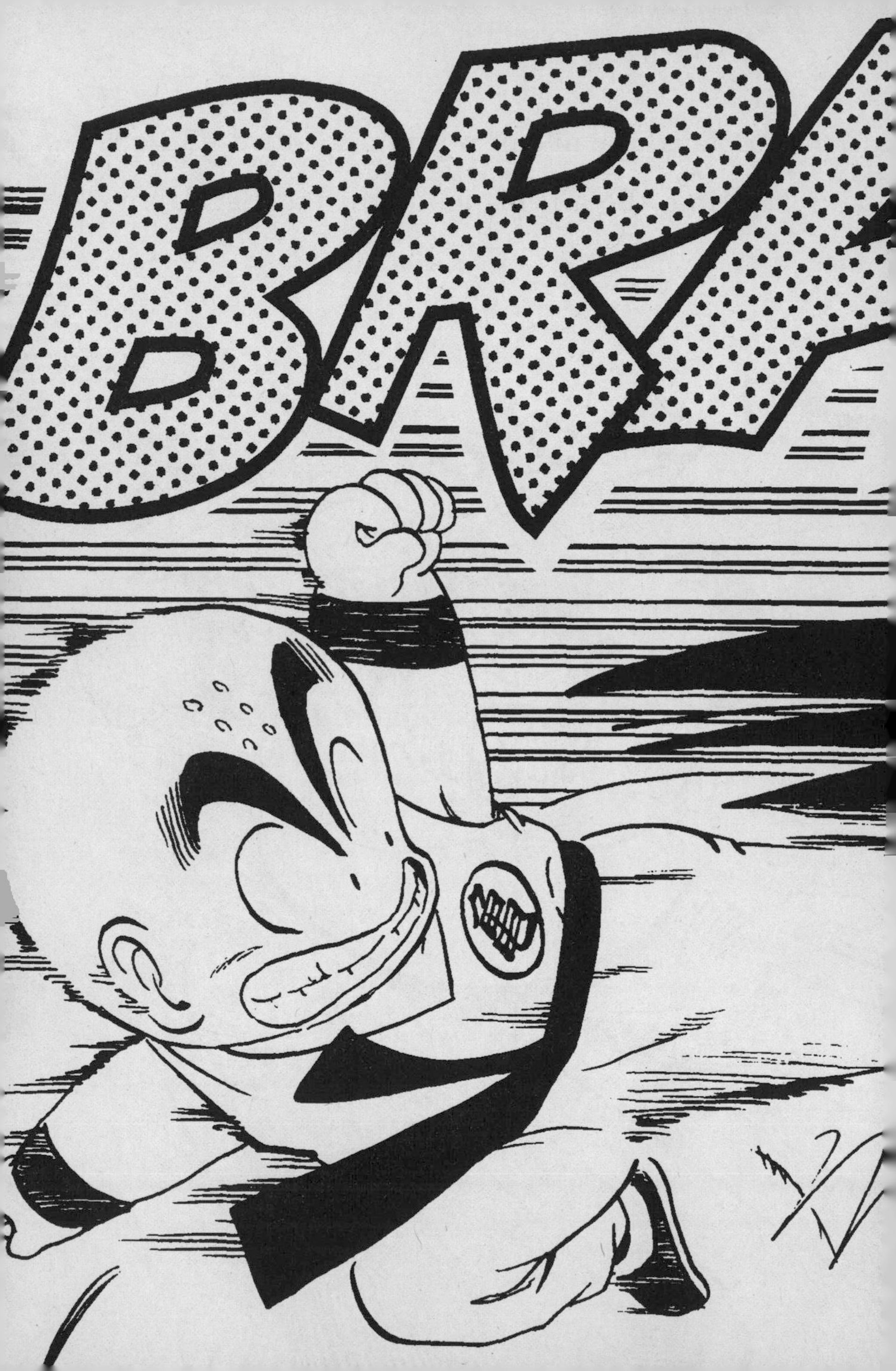
BAM

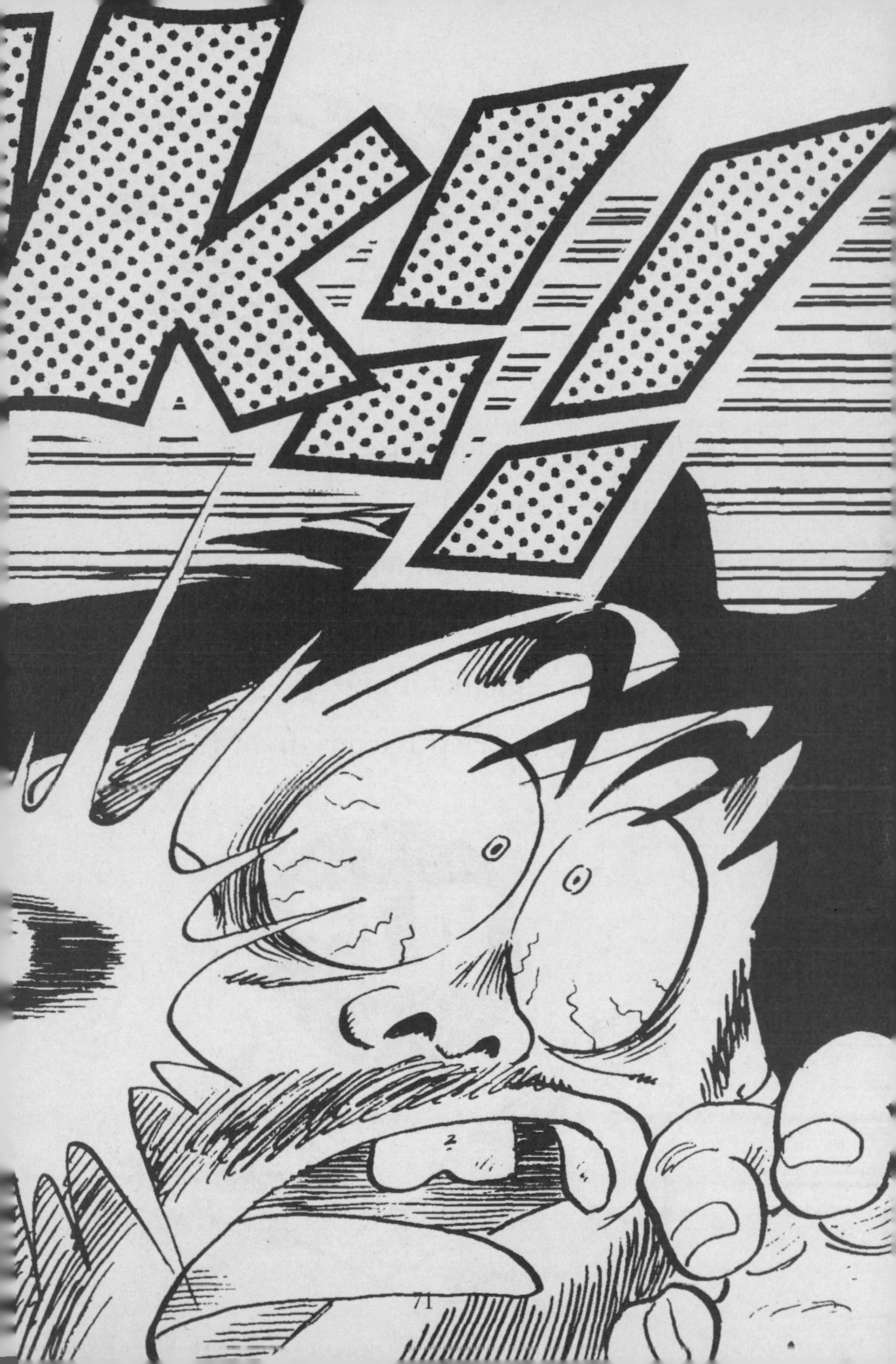

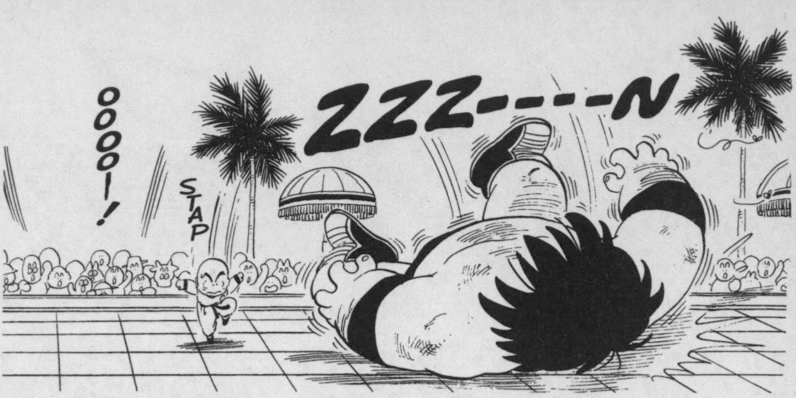
OOOOO!!
STAP
ZZZ----N

Krillin's kick knocked the festering giant off his feet. Krillin ran toward Bacterian and climbed his massive chest to his shoulder. Then Krillin turned, squatted and–BLLAAP!–gave Bacterian a little something to remember him by.

"M-m-mercy!" cried Bacterian. "Mercy!"

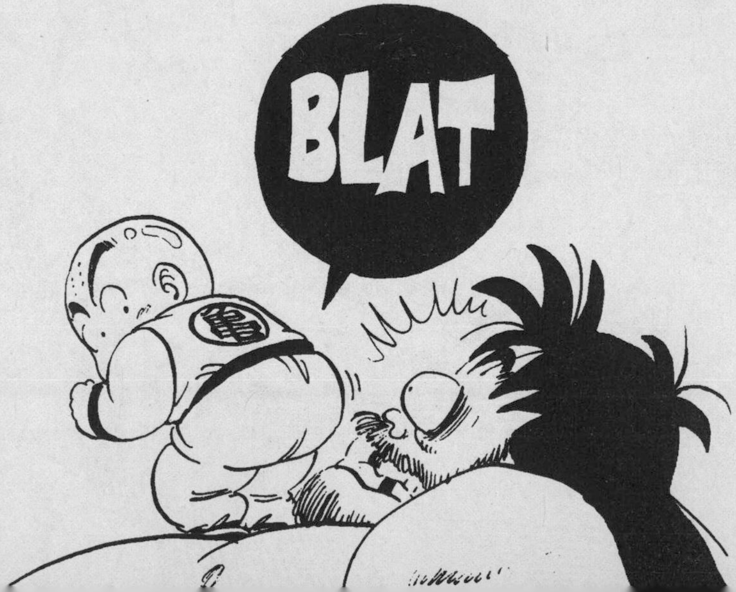
BLAT

The crowd went wild. Goku rushed to the stage and raised Krillin's hand in victory.

"What a comeback!" the announcer cried. "What a magnificent victory for Krillin…the boy with no nose!"

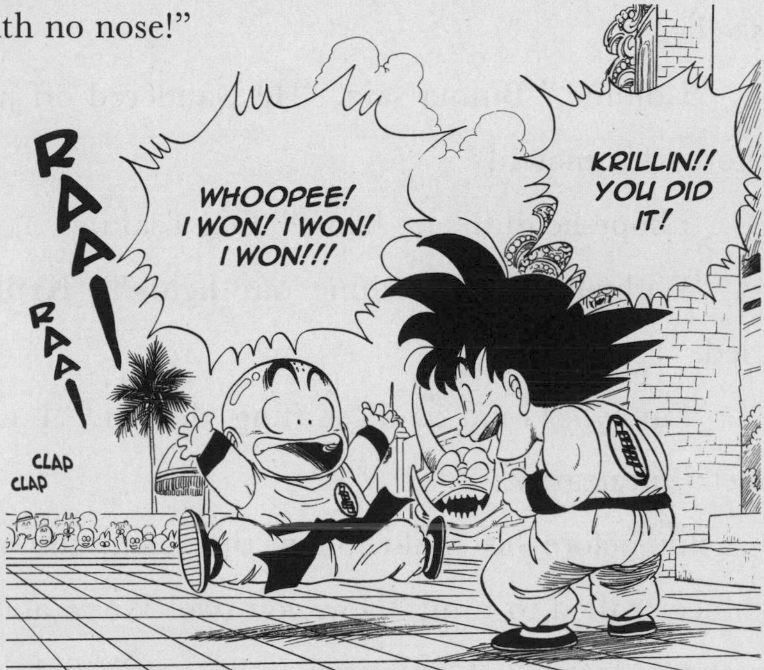
KRILLIN!! YOU DID IT!
WHOOPEE! I WON! I WON! I WON!!!
RAAA!
RAAA!
CLAP
CLAP

"Krillin, you did it!!" yelled Goku.

"I won!" Krillin breathed, still in a daze. "I won I won I won!!"

"I wonder if ol' Turtle Guy was watching!" Goku laughed.

"I sure hope so!" Krillin replied.

They ran to find their friends in the stands, but they saw only Bulma, Oolong, and Pu'ar.

"But...but where's Master Roshi?" Krillin asked.

"I dunno," Bulma said. "He wandered off just before your match!"

"I hope he didn't go home!" Goku said.

"Without even watching our fights?!" Krillin cried.

"Funny," Goku said, sniffing the air. "I can smell him nearby..."

But before he could follow the scent, the announcer called to him: "Hey, you two! We're about to start Match 2. Contestants who aren't fighting have to wait inside."

"'Kay," said Goku quietly, and he followed Krillin back into the hall.

"Ladies and gentlemen," they heard the announcer say over the loud speaker, "Match 2 is about to begin. Jackie Chun and Yamcha, please step forward!"

Yamcha strode toward the door, tossing a grin at Goku. "Well, I guess I'm up!"

"Good luck, Yamcha!" Goku said.

Jackie Chun stood slowly and strolled to the door. He stopped in front of Krillin and said, "That was a magnificent kick, young man."

"Oh! Thanks very much!" Krillin said. He watched Jackie Chun stroll toward the door. "Strange," he said. "I feel like I know that guy from somewhere..."

But Krillin had no time to wonder—Match 2 was about to begin!

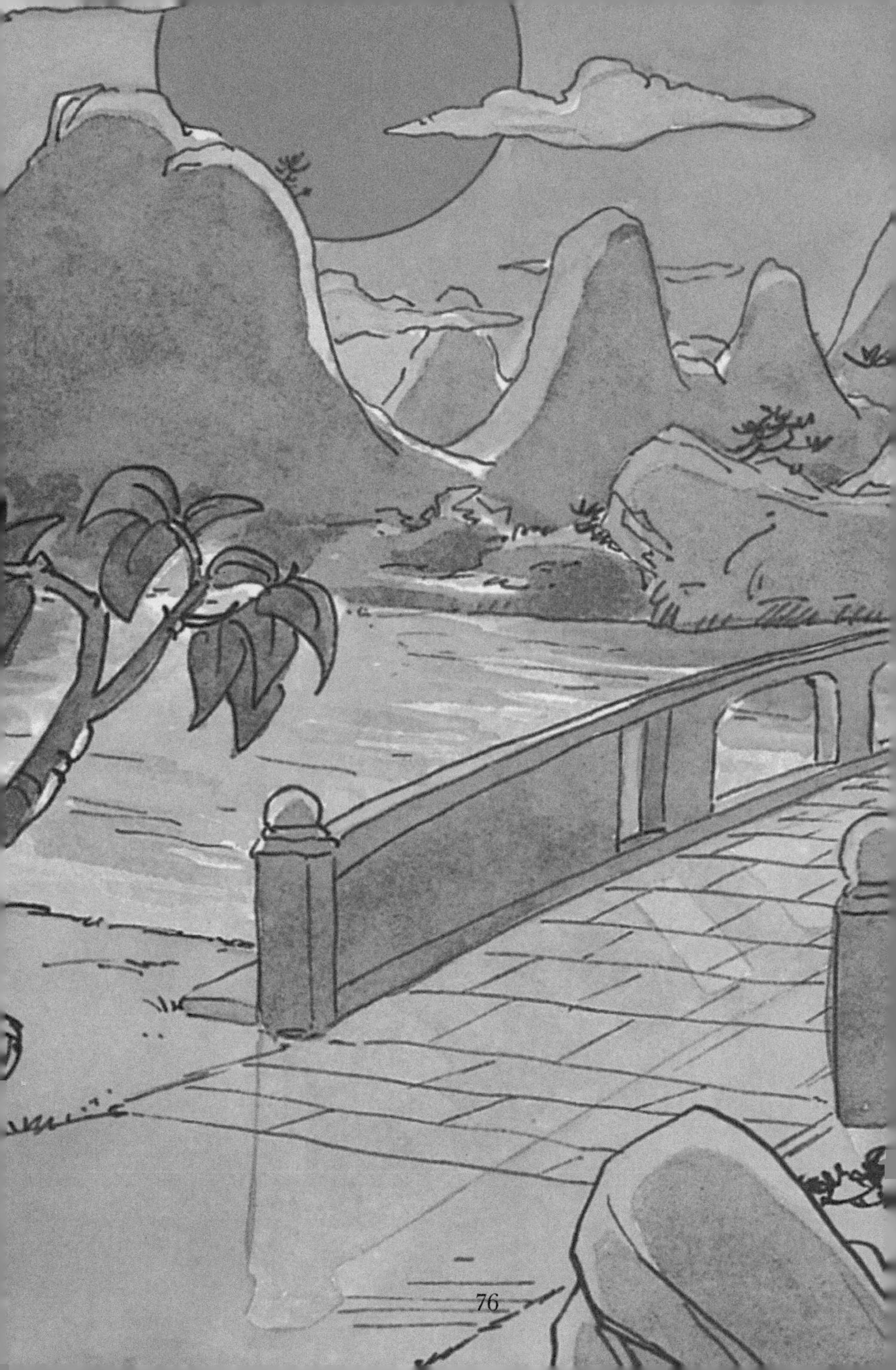

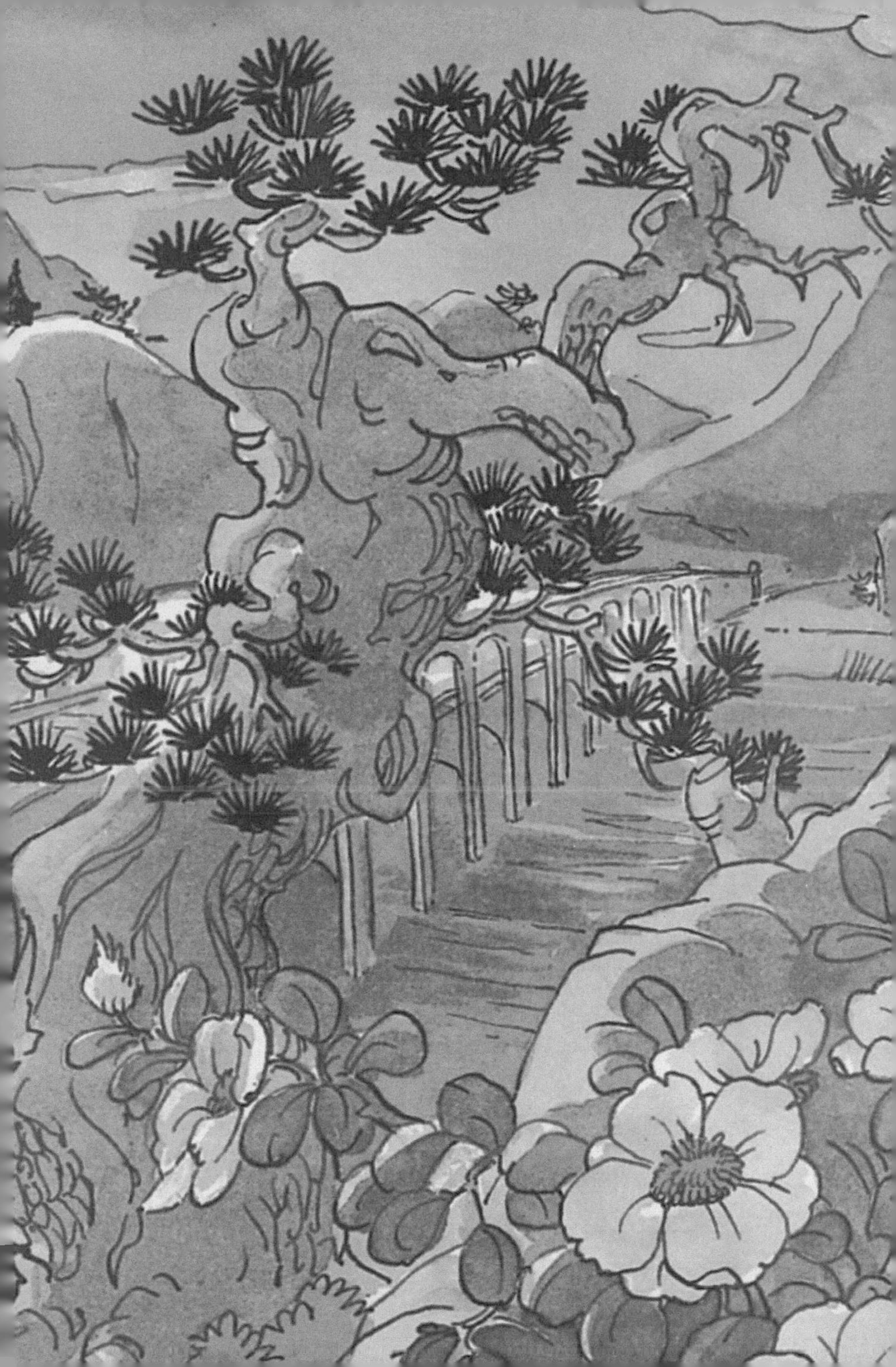

Glossary

Dragon Ball: one of seven mythical orbs that when brought together have the power to summon a wish-granting dragon

Fist of the Wolf Fang: Yamcha's signature move in which he uses wolf-like speed and power to defeat his opponent

Kinto'un: a flying cloud that will carry only those who are pure of heart

Stink-Fu: Bacterian's signature fighting move in which he uses his stink to overcome his opponents

A Note About Bacterian

We all know that good hygiene is important for staying healthy, but what would really happen if, like Bacterian, you never, ever bathed?

First, let's talk about bacteria. Bacteria are microscopic creatures with lots of different jobs. Some keep you healthy. Others make things rot. And some can cause serious infections. Bathing helps protect you from bad bacteria and other things that can make you sick, which means Bacterian must be crawling with gross.

For example, hair that's never been washed would probably be swarming with lice, tiny bugs that like to eat skin and drink blood. A never-washed face is an open invitation to a bacterial infection called Trachoma, which can cause blindness. A fungus called ringworm and tiny, itchy bugs called scabies love dirty skin. Some of these things are very easy to pass from one person to another, so if Bacterian were a real guy, there'd be far more to worry about than his terrible smell.

And about that smell... Bacterian's personal perfume is the scent of bacteria growing on his body. These odor-causing critters do best in warm, sweaty places like feet and armpits.

Who wants to wash their hands?

About the Authors

Akira Toriyama
Original Creator of the *Dragon Ball* Manga

Artist/writer Akira Toriyama burst onto the manga (Japanese comics) scene in 1980, with the wildly popular *Dr. Slump*, a science fiction comedy about the adventures of a mad scientist and his android daughter. In 1984 he created the beloved series *Dragon Ball,* which has been translated into many languages, and, as a series, has sold over 150 million copies in Japan. Toriyama-san lives with his family in Japan.

Gerard Jones
Dragon Ball Chapter Book Author

Gerard Jones has been adapting Japanese manga for English-speaking audiences since 1989, including the entire run of *Dragon Ball* comics for VIZ Media and the *Pokémon* comic strip for Creators Syndicate (reprinted by VIZ as *Pikachu Meets the Press*). He has also written hundreds of original comic books for Marvel, DC, and other publishers, and he is the author of several books on popular culture and children's media, including *Killing Monsters* and the Eisner Award-winning *Men of Tomorrow*. He lives in San Francisco with his wife and son, where he works and teaches at the San Francisco Writers Grotto.

Coming Soon...

Book Eight
FIGHT TO THE FINISH!

The matches are getting tougher and tougher as the fighting moves become more and more astounding! Will Goku survive Giran's gooey gut gum? Will Krillin be undone by Jackie Chun? Who is this Jackie Chun guy anyway? And why is he leading everyone in a sing-along? Oh, it's a strange time at the Tenkaichi Budokai tonight!

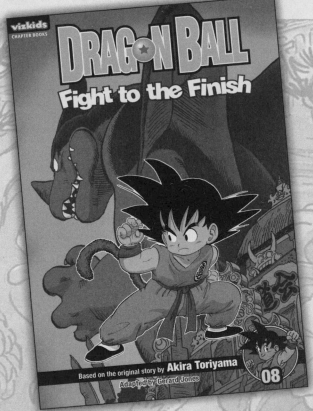